Like Sisters on the Homefront

RITA WILLIAMS-GARCIA

PUFFIN BOOKS

PUFFIN BOOKS
Published by the Penguin Group
Penguin Putnam Inc., 375 Hudson Street, New York, New York 10014, U.S.A.
Penguin Books Ltd, 27 Wrights Lane, London W8 5TZ, England
Penguin Books Australia Ltd, Ringwood, Victoria, Australia
Penguin Books Canada Ltd, 10 Alcorn Avenue, Toronto, Ontario, Canada M4V 3B2
Penguin Books (N.Z.) Ltd, 182-190 Wairau Road, Auckland 10, New Zealand

Penguin Books Ltd, Registered Offices: Harmondsworth, Middlesex, England

First published in the United States of America by Lodestar Books,
an affiliate of Dutton Children's Books, a division of Penguin Books USA Inc., 1995
Published in Puffin Books, 1997

10 9 8

THE LIBRARY OF CONGRESS HAS CATALOGED THE LODESTAR EDITION AS FOLLOWS:
Williams-Garcia, Rita.
Like sisters on the homefront/Rita Williams-Garcia—1st ed.
  p. cm.
Summary: Troubled fourteen-year-old Gayle is sent down South to live
with her uncle and aunt, where her life begins to change as she
experiences the healing power of the family.
ISBN 0-525-67465-9
[1. Afro-Americans—Fiction. 2. Family life—Fiction.]
I. Title.
PZ7.W6714Li 1995 [Fic]—dc20 95-3690 CIP AC

Puffin Books ISBN 0-14-038561-4

Printed in the United States of America

*for Alana, Michelle, Stephanie,
and especially Elaine Isaacs,
who made this work possible*

🌮1🌮

THE FIRST TIME Gayle slammed the bathroom door, her mother let it go. The second time, Mama's ears perked up, listening for familiar sounds. The third time Gayle ran into the bathroom, Mama was up the stairs and on Gayle's heels, witnessing what she already knew. Gayle, stooped over the toilet bowl, face flushed, body heaving, was pregnant. Again.

Mama snatched a paper cup from the dispenser and almost crushed it. She filled the cup with tap water, thrust it at Gayle's mouth, and ordered her to gargle and spit. For once, Gayle did as she was told, then wiped her lips, thinking, No use breaking into a story. Mama already knew.

Ow!

Gayle rubbed her hot cheek, keeping the hurt to herself. If anything, she felt a chuckle bubbling underneath the sting of Mama's slap. Sensing that Mama was hardly in the mood for fun and games, Gayle wisely kept it to herself as well.

Mama splashed a handful of cold water on Gayle's face and dabbed it with a towel. "You far 'long?" she asked, then sought her own answer by patting Gayle's belly.

1

Gayle shrugged. "You clean? Did you bathe?" Before Gayle could respond, Mama added, "Then dress the baby, 'cause we going."

"Where we going?" Gayle asked, excited that Mama was taking action. Mama was something else when she was wound up for war. Oooh, bet we going to Troy's house, Gayle thought. Have it out with Troy Mama.

"Where we going?" Gayle asked again.

Mama repeated, "We going," with an eerie determination that made Gayle anticipate fireworks at Troy's house.

Gayle stood in the hallway, listening to her mother's telephone conversation. Judging by Mama's humble demeanor, Gayle ruled out Troy's mama as the other party. She heard "... No, it's not Junie. It's Gayle ..." follow by three "Yes, Miz Feldmans" in Mama's best "work voice." Then she heard the receiver slam. Now Mama was angry because she had to sound like a child begging permission to take care of business.

Gayle fled into her bedroom to avoid hearing what she had cost Mama. She sat on her bed, where her son lay on his back kicking his fat, buttermilk-colored legs wildly, celebrating her return. She fought the urge to smile at him, not wanting him to get the idea that this was play-time. José was being obstinate this morning. Curling his toes so she couldn't slip the soft shoes on. "Hold still," she told him. He kicked his feet. "Why you gotta act so stupid?" she scolded and smacked his toes a little so he'd know: STOP PLAYING AROUND. It worked. His wet little mouth made a perfect O, and he let out suspenseful breaths. "For seven months you ain't too stupid."

Gayle tied her own sneakers then put her son on her too narrow hip. Down the stairs she trooped, hoping the thunder would end Junie's sleep.

Mama was at the door. "I gave you your one mistake," she said. "Thought you'd learn something."

Junior rolled over on the sofa and blinked until his eyes stayed open. "She belly out again? It was Troy, wasn't it?"

Mama turned her attention to the sofa. "Junie, go to work and stop minding everybody's business."

Junie swore he'd hurt Troy first chance he got.

For being eighteen and out of school, Junie still had a lot of kid in him. He was always into some low-level trouble. Nothing that would get him put away, but always busy trying. Mouthing off, getting into fights, selling things that obviously weren't his—prompting strangers to come knocking on the door at two and three o'clock in the morning hunting him down, while he lay on the sofa faking a coma and leaving Mama to deal with them.

Junie rolled back into a fetal position and closed his eyes. Junie was Mama's favorite 'cause he had his daddy's face on him. As far as Gayle was concerned, Daddy could stay dead if that's what he looked like. Junie made her sick. Mama let Junie lay up in the house doing nothing while Gayle did all the housework. Gayle sneered at him, thinking, Junie gon' be a punk boy all his life. Her consolation was that she would be a woman for the rest of hers.

Gayle strapped the baby into the stroller and lifted the stroller down the porch stairs. Before leaving, Mama issued another warning for Junie to unpeel himself from the sofa, though Mama and Gayle knew it was fruitless.

Mama was walking awfully fast. They seemed to be going the wrong way. Weren't they going to Troy Mama house so they could start some fireworks?

"We not going to Troy's?"

"For what? Troy already stuck in his two cents. That's what you carrying. Troy's two cents."

"Where we going?"

"Women's Clinic."

"For what?" Gayle asked.

"Don't be cute. Cute got you where you at."

"S'pose I want to keep it. It's mines."

"As long as you fourteen and in *my* house, you mines," Mama said. "Only one woman in my house. I say what goes on in my four walls—and I'm not having it. What you think I'm running? Does my door say South Jamaica Welfare Hotel? No. Do you see Hoe House on my mailbox? No. It say 150-11 South Road. Have the nerve to say 'Whitaker' on the welcome mat."

Gayle giggled, then laughed out loud. "See, Mama. You be pissing me off and making me laugh at the same time."

Mama kept up her pace. "Laugh now," she said. "The joke won't be on me and it damn sure won't be on you. Not while I'm living."

When they got to the Women's Clinic on Sutphin Boulevard, the lady said Gayle didn't have to have no abortion against her will. Mama couldn't force her on the table. She used words like *choice, consent, coercion,* and some other big *c* words. She was white, but young like a college girl. No makeup. No hairstyle. Looked like she been studying all night long. Had her schoolbook open at the desk with yellow highlighter streaks all through it.

Mama could care less for the college girl look. Mama smacked her in the face with some southside talk. Stomped her into the ground with one of those vicious "Mama glares," all 'cause she a little white girl using big *c* words to make Mama look like a caged gorilla. Boy, Mama could show out!

When Ruby Whitaker spit out the last of her wrath, that white girl didn't utter another *c* word. Didn't look up. Just signed Gayle in, told mother and daughter to have a seat in the room till Gayle's name was called, and went back to marking up her schoolbook in yellow highlighter.

They made the mistake—judging by Mama's expression—of sitting next to a young woman who told Gayle right away, "I'm having an abortion and a tubal ligation." She was much older than Gayle. Early twenties, at least.

Gayle wrinkled her nose, not liking the sound of it. "What's that?" she asked.

"When they tie your tubes so you don't have no more babies. Only takes a minute. See, this 'bout my sev—no eighth—pregnancy. I got four kids at home. Had some abortions, lost some. How 'bout you?"

Gayle didn't know if she meant pregnancy or abortion. "I just got this here baby," she said, pointing to José, who had discovered the jingle bells fastened to his shoelaces and was kicking his legs excitedly. "And this one." She meant the one in her belly. Mama grunted.

Gayle eyed some Hispanics across the room. She assumed they were a pregnant girl, her mama, and her boyfriend. They were praying and crying—the boy and the mama doing most of it while the girl consoled them.

Everyone else was just waiting, biting lips, turning paler, staring at posters but not reading them. At fourteen, Gayle was hardly the youngest in the room. She saw all kinds of black girls, white girls, Hispanic girls, and Asian girls. There was an East Indian–looking girl with perfect brown skin and a ponytail long enough to sit on. Gayle imagined herself with that long ponytail, then snapped out of it. The thought of being dragged around the schoolyard by the hair was not pleasant, as Gayle was always starting something with the biggest gal she could find.

A woman wearing a blue-and-white RESPECT LIFE button pinned to her sweater and a gold crucifix around her neck came in and identified herself as a counselor. She said that life was a gift and that there were other options besides abortion, such as adoption. She described the loving environment each child would have, and the nice TV family that would adopt the child and raise it to one day be president. She said that anyone who decided to have her baby would be entitled to prenatal care, the opportunity to finish school, and job training.

Without parting her lips, Mama telegraphed, "Get that thought out your head 'fore I smack it out."

Gayle glanced up at her mother and snickered, figuring since Mama had ruined her chances of hooking Troy, she would get back at her mother by saying to the Tube-Tying Woman, "That 'doption sounds good," all the while knowing it was hype. Ain't nobody breaking they necks to adopt black babies.

Out of a dozen, two girls couldn't discern the "hype." They leaped to their feet, choosing adoption, and followed the RESPECT LIFE lady into another room.

A nurse came in to explain the procedure. Gayle grew impatient with the nurse's concern that they understand everything. Gayle didn't want to understand. She just wanted to get it over with.

Finally, those who wanted to go ahead followed the nurse into another room. The one girl who kept holding things up by asking questions wanted to call her mother. Gayle and the Tube-Tying Woman shared furtive glances, knowing the girl on the phone wasn't going ahead.

They were now on their own. No mamas. No boyfriends. No sisters. No girlfriends. Just pregnant girls. Some pregnant women. Bare legs and paper gowns. One after another, submitting to exams. Gayle passed. Six weeks pregnant. Another girl was told to come back in two weeks. It was too early to do anything. She was crying about how hard it was to get there. That she had come a long, long way. Couldn't they just do it? They said no. Then she started rolling around on the cold floor in that paper gown like a little kid having a sugar fit. Even when they took her out, Gayle could still hear her tinny teenage voice screaming, "Pleeese! Pleeese!"

The Tube-Tying Woman, who struck Gayle as being goosey, suddenly adjusted her tone. "Someone should watch that girl. No telling what she might do." The Tube-Tying Woman said she had seen this all the time. "Girls wind up trying to do it theyselves. Mess theyselves up for life or bleed to death."

It was time. Big-armed nurses in aqua uniforms came in every ten minutes to load up the gurneys and push them left or right. The Tube-Tying Woman was the first to go.

There was a woman doctor and a man doctor. Gayle didn't want no woman doctor getting into her eggs and fish cakes. She thought, Womens shouldn't be touching womens down there. How do you know they not jealous 'cause you young and can have babies while they gotta work and be doctors 'cause they can't get a man?

Good. Man doctor.

He looked at her chart to see what kind of anesthesia she wanted. He looked twice, then asked if she was sure the local. Mama had already told Gayle she had to be awake. They didn't have extra money for sleep.

Gayle figured since she had already toughed it out with birthing José she could deal with local anesthesia. It wasn't as if she could die from the pain. And the doctor was so nice. West Indian guy. He talked to her with her knees up and her feet in the cold stirrups like it was nothing. Gayle said she was ready once they gave her the needle. She wanted to see it happening, but the doctor

7

said she had to be still. She felt some pumping and some pinching. Whooooooooo. That local wasn't kicking in like she thought it would. She made a fist, then cursed Mama for not having enough money for sleep. The doctor told her she was brave. "Oh, Doc, it ain't nothing to cry about," she said. When it was over she asked if she could see what he put in the metal pan. He said it wasn't nothing to see.

Gayle remembered the gurney rolling again but couldn't remember being helped into her clothes or into her chair. She searched the narrow room, noting familiar faces—minus the two who had chosen adoption, the one who had asked for her mama, and the one the clinic had turned away. They had all made it. The Tube-Tying Woman wanted to leave and pick up her children from day care. The East Indian girl combed her long ponytail with her fingers and stared at her feet. The Hispanic girl comforted an Asian girl, who was also staring at her feet. When the girls' eyes left their feet or the tiles or the posters, they found each other and conveyed their relief and concern.

A nurse wheeling a tray of orange juice stopped to pour Gayle a cup. Gayle took it, feeling the nurse resisting the urge to shake her head um, um, um.

A counselor came in and stood at the front. To keep from catching the reflective glare of her too shiny, too round glasses Gayle focused on her huge blue-and-white button that said RESPECT YOURSELF! Gayle craved a cigarette, a stick of gum. She needed something to bite on while the counselor went on and on about self-esteem, self-control, birth control, keeping clean, cotton panties, and no nookie for six weeks. Restless, the Tube-Tying Woman took advantage of every joke-cracking opportunity.

The counselor suggested with true sincerity, "Have someone else do the housework."

"You lending out your maid?"

"Have someone else watch the children."

"A maid and a nanny," cried the Tube-Tying Woman. "Say, lady, that's some life you living!"

Then the counselor insisted, "Absolutely no strenuous exercise during the next six weeks. No jogging."

The Tube-Tying Woman did not need to say a word. Everyone hollered with laughter, including the counselor.

When she emerged through the side door, Gayle found her mother waiting anxiously with the stroller. She peered down into the stroller and smiled at her son, noting that single-mindedness must run in the family. José had finally kicked off his shoe and was worn out by his efforts.

"You all right?" Mama asked.

Gayle tilted her head, lifted her eyebrows, and released a sigh. "Guesso."

Mama said the cab would be there any minute, but that was all she said. They looked off in opposite directions as they waited. Mama wouldn't give Gayle room to vent her feelings about her ordeal and Gayle wasn't about to volunteer the details of her pains.

∾ 2 ∾

GAYLE called Troy Mama house every half hour and let the phone ring fifteen times before she hung up. On her fourth try, Troy Mama answered the phone and said her son wasn't home so stop calling and worrying her to death. Gayle said it was important. Could she *please* tell Troy—then Troy Mama cut her off quick. "Look here, miss. I know which one you are. You're that pale, skinny child always in my living room starting up business every time I turn around. If Troy wants to find you, let him find you. If he ain't scout you out, take the hint."

Thwarted, Gayle mashed down the receiver, cutting short the other woman's "problem with you gals today" litany. She placed the phone on the nightstand and smoothed out the wrinkles on Mama's bedspread before returning to her room.

The locked-in mustiness of her own bedroom was strong, particularly after having left Mama's clean, lilac-scented room. It wasn't just the smell of her sloth sealed in by July heat, but all that it signified. Being trapped. Missing out. While all that good old dirt was kicking up out there, she had been inside for the past two days changing diapers and listening to José scream and carry on because Mama had ordered her to stay in her room. If it were left up to Mama, Gayle wouldn't set foot on concrete heaven until she was too old to care. All that talk about "resting and healing" was Mama's cover-up for "Stay yo' shiny yella heinie behind bars."

Enough was enough, Gayle decided. She had healed all she was gonna heal outside of a little spotting and some cramping. She bathed José, then dressed and fed him, strapped him into his stroller, got dressed, laced her sneakers, and left without washing her face.

Times like these called for getting with the homegirls and trashing both Mama and Troy Mama for hours on end. With spirits rising, they'd move on to Gayle's adventures at the Women's Clinic. How they'd marvel at Gayle's ability to laugh about her experience. In minutes she would have them dying over hilarious accounts of the girl at the desk, the counselors, the doctors, and the women waiting—especially the Tube-Tying Woman.

The southside homegirls. Tight since day care, holding on through junior high. Winning double Dutch jump-offs. Ditching Bible studies, study hall, and ballet classes. Protecting one anothers' secrets and lies, yet always quick to "read" one another when necessary. Lynda, Terri, and Gayle. Sometimes Joycie. Like sisters on the homefront, looking out for one another. All Gayle needed was to get with the girls, get with the girls . . .

She rang Lynda's doorbell only to discover she had missed her by five minutes. Lynda Mama kept Lynda busy with a baby-sitting job across town followed by track and field with the Police Athletic League. During the school year, Gayle and Terri would go to Lynda's track meets to cheer her on. Fine guys with muscles and colored trunks would be there flexing and strutting and calling out to Lynda, "Yo, baby, yo, lightning" 'cause Lynda was fast.

The homegirls would hook up Lynda's braids with red and yellow beads so she'd look wicked rounding those turns in the relays.

Lynda was not the only fast one. Gayle was fast too. She could have been in track and field. In fact, she tried out for the hundred-meter hurdles when José was a tadpole in her stomach upsetting her Rice Krispies in the morning. Like she told the track coach, who thought she had talent, "Kinda hard making that hurdle when you have a baby in your belly."

Gayle didn't bother with Joycie's doorbell since Joycie wouldn't be home the whole summer. Joycie Mama, Miss Minnie Collins, let Joycie go to Africa with her dance troupe to study real deal bush dancing. It was written up in the *Amsterdam News*, the *City Sun*, and all those black papers.

Gayle could have been a dancer too. Not like Joycie. No one could touch Joycie. It wouldn't surprise Gayle if Joycie came back with stories of them Africans trying to make her their queen.

Terri's corner house was her last hope before turning around and going home. Terri's house was the only one on the block guarded by an iron fence. Gayle unlatched the gate and pushed the stroller in and up the walkway. Terri didn't have a lot of talent for dancing onstage or clearing high hurdles, but Terri was reliable. Gayle could always depend on Terri to watch José while she went over to Troy's.

Gayle pushed the doorbell. No one answered. She rang the bell again. Again. Again. Maybe Terri was asleep. Terri often didn't get up until noon, so Gayle searched for a stone small enough to throw up to her window.

"All right, all right. Who that ringing my bell?" It was Terri Granny.

"It's me, Gayle. Terri up?"

"Up? Up? She up and outta here to school." Terri Granny stuck her head out, then back in. She looked like a hen.

"School?"

"Summer school or get left back," quipped Terri Granny. "Seems like you could use some more schooling."

"Puh-leez. September be here soon enough."

"Look like you needs something. Got too much time on your hands and nothing going on upstairs and that says one thing. Trouble."

"I ain't in no trouble. That be Junie causing a ruckus."

"I heard about you. Up to your navel in quicksand," Terri Granny said.

Why everybody gotta be in my A to Z? "I asked for Terri, not a lecture, Granny. Just tell her to call me. It's important."

Terry Granny muttered something about a private secretary then closed the door in Gayle's face.

"Well, excuse me!" Gayle fumed. "Talk about rude."

She pushed the stroller down the walkway and stood outside the iron gate. Not a one of them home, she thought. Not a one.

This felt worse than being left hanging by Troy or José's father. Part of the fun of not knowing when she'd next see them was in adding yet another episode to the soap opera when either one of them did materialize. But being without the girls, her sisters, was being cut off from life itself. Without her girls to hang with or provide amusement she was genuinely lost. Her imagination didn't tell her to board a bus or subway train to see what was out there beyond her block, the Forty Projects, and Jamaica Avenue. She couldn't go but so far, anyway. The little traveling she did made her cramp up and she felt herself spotting blood. "Now why didn't I strap on some Kotex?" she asked. José couldn't tell her. He could only drool.

She wheeled the stroller to the park and sat down, hoping someone she knew would wander through. Luckily she had had the sense to pack a jar of baby food and a bottle of juice since José was starting up his "feed me" nonsense again.

Full and content, José dozed off for his noontime nap. It would have been nice if he had stayed awake long enough to play. As it was, Gayle sat without a book or magazine to read, a Walkman to listen to, or a soul to hear her tale. She came desperately close to flagging down a friend of an acquaintance but decided the girl was too far away.

With her foot hooked underneath the stroller basket, she rolled the stroller back and forth and stared beyond the greenish brown pond and the soccer field, over to the other side of Baisley Park. José's father and his family lived across the park. She, Terri, and Lynda used to venture over to the other side of the park and sit there waiting for José's wife, Gloria, to come out. Lynda and Terri were supposed to hold Gloria down while Gayle stomped on her. The one time Gloria did come out, Gayle saw that she wasn't the old, old woman who José said had tricked him into marriage. Gloria was about José's age, nineteen or twenty.

Soon the yellow jackets and pond mosquitoes drawn in by the fruity smell of José's lunch forced Gayle out of the park. She wheeled her stroller home. At least there she could catch the soaps on TV until Terri and Lynda came home.

Shoot. Mama home. Must not have gone to work. Junie still on the couch as usual. Figures.

Gayle lifted her son out of the stroller and snuck

upstairs to her room. Her mattress had been stripped and the blinds and windows were raised as high as they could go. When she stuck her hand in her top dresser drawer to rummage for Kotex her fingertips drummed wood grain. She looked in the drawer. Empty. Every one of her dresser drawers had been cleaned out. She pulled out the bottom drawer used for José's clothes. Empty. She opened her closet doors. Only winter clothes. Mama had gone crazy and was exorcising her room.

"We'll see about this," she said, putting José in his crib. "All she gotta say is 'Clean your room' and I'll clean it. She don't gotta be going through all these changes."

Gayle trotted downstairs looking for answers. She shook her brother. "Junie. Junie." He opened his eyes, saw his sister, cussed, and rolled over. She smacked him lightly on the head. That was when she noticed a cheap plaid suitcase and two A & P shopping bags standing next to the TV.

She heard Mama's footsteps marching heavily up the basement steps. She sped into the kitchen to meet her.

"Where my clothes?"

Mama calmly pointed in the direction of the TV.

"You puttin' us out?"

Still calm, Mama shook her head. "I'm packing you up and sending you home."

"Home? Home?" And it registered. She knew exactly where "home" was. Mama, that Junie-loving, good-time-killing cow, meant down Souf. "I ain't goin' down there," Gayle declared, forgetting herself. Forgetting you don't tell Mama what you "ain't" doing, certainly not with your neck snaking figure eights. "Unh-unh," she resumed, louder. "And if you think I'm leaving my man and my friends you crazier'n I thought."

"You'll find out just *how* crazy . . . keep talking." Mama took a step forward.

With nothing to lose, Gayle said, "We gon' find out 'cause I ain't going." She went along with the abortion because she could always have another baby. But now Mama was talking crazy. She was supposed to give up her friends and her man without a squawk.

"Don't try me," Mama sang, her voice frightfully unstable.

"Well I'm trying," Gayle said, taking the final step. And that did it. Neither could back down.

Junie sprang from the sofa to get Mama off of Gayle. As Mama turned to get the best of Junie, Gayle took her opportunity to fly upstairs and lock her door.

She needed to get to the phone in Mama's room, but with Mama raging downstairs, wild enough to turn on Junie no less, Gayle didn't dare leave her room. Her girls. How was she going to get to her girls? One word to them, they'd knock on Troy Mama house. Then Troy be up here quick. And when he finds out it was Mama who made her scrape out his baby he'll turn this place inside out with some sho 'nuf fireworks.

Gayle took José from his crib and lay him on the mattress next to her. She fondled his curls and put her thumb in her mouth and stared at the ceiling until she fell asleep on the stripped-down mattress.

❧ 3 ❧

WHOEVER *heard of going to the airport on a bus? You s'posed to go in a taxi or in somebody car. We traveling on a bus with a suitcase and shopping bags. Then gotta walk ten miles through the parking lot 'cause Mama too cheap to spring for a cab.*

Gayle struggled, grumbled, and occasionally glared at Mama, who moved through the parked cars like a bulldozer.

José, joined to his mother's waist and chest by a cloth carrier, blew raspberries and babbled new sounds. He loved being outdoors, the rocking motion of his mother's gait, and the vibrant thump of her heartbeat. His mommy, his mommy, his mommy, his mommy.

Gayle wondered when it would end. When she could rest. When he would learn to walk. All seventeen pounds of him strained her back, while her baby bag loaded down with baby supplies—not to mention José's "bankie"—oppressed her shoulders.

How could she make it with her back bent and her legs heavy with exhaustion? Even Rasheeda Davis could maneuver better. Rasheeda Davis was the only physically handicapped eighth-grader at her school. Struggling with

17

her load, Gayle could use a tip from Rasheeda Davis, who continued to excel in school in spite of her leg braces.

No use seeking sympathy from Mama on how heavy José was. Mama kept stories in reserve for such occasions about toting Gayle in one arm and Junie in the other because he was so sickly. Besides, Mama was already carrying the two shopping bags, suitcase, and her big old pocketbook full of all that money she wouldn't give Gayle but would pour on Junie 'cause Junie her precious son, which didn't faze Gayle 'cause one day Gayle would get her own money and spend it all on her son and not toss Mama a rusty, crusty penny.

"Why we couldn't take the stroller?" Gayle wailed, shifting José to one side. "How'm I gonna get around with no stroller?"

"You won't need a stroller. Just keep still 'steada flying here and there. Flying is what got you where you at."

"Yeah. At a airport," Gayle said.

They walked between the yellow cabs lined up against the curb and went inside the terminal. Not once did Mama seek out an accommodating face for directions, as if the details of the trip had been fixed in her mind for some time. She and Gayle went straight to the right line, got up to the right counter, paid with Mama's credit card, went through the metal detector, and sat outside the boarding gate.

Gayle wanted a soda and a sweetcake before getting on the plane. Mama said to wait for the plane snack because they charge you double in airport shops. From that point on Mama didn't stop talking. Not about anything Gayle could appreciate, such as missing her or José, or calming Gayle's fear of flying, but about dos and don'ts. Mostly don'ts.

"*Don't* be starting no stuff. Brother won't put up with any coming and going and talking out the side of your face. *Do* act like you know better, y'hear. *Don't* be eatin' up all their food and lying around watching TV, and *don't* be dragging when they call. *Don't* get on their phone calling up the world. I'll reach out and light you up long distance if I hear of it. *Do* speak up when you're spoken to, and *do* call grown people Miss So-and-So and Mr. So-and-So." Don't, don't. Do, do.

"Dog," Gayle groaned. "That's it? I'm the slave girl?"

"There's a connection in Charlotte with an hour layover," Mama went on. "*Don't* go wandering around. Above all, *do* be where you s'posed to be. And *don't* miss that flight calling me talking about 'oops.' I'll oops you into tomorrow. And *don't*—and I do mean *don't*—find your way back to my doorstep till you're sent for."

Like everything else in her fourteen-year-old life, Gayle had no say. When José was born Mama filled out the birth certificate application at the hospital on account of Gayle's poor spelling and her general confusion with written instructions. Instead of listing José Cortez as the father Mama wrote "Father Unknown." Instead of listing the baby's name as José Emanuel Cortez, Mama wrote "Emanuel Gates Whitaker." *Gates? That's a part of a fence, not a name.* In spite of Gayle's protests, Emanuel Gates Whitaker stuck to all the papers that later followed. Just like the abortion, the baby's name, and now the airplane going south, Gayle had no say.

She could see the mighty white bird on the runway. She had never been on an airplane. To Gayle, traveling involved a bus pass to destinations close enough to walk back from if necessary. The farthest she had ventured out of South Jamaica was going to a rap concert at Yankee Stadium up in the Bronx with Troy. The thought of being thousands of miles in the air where birds didn't fly was not appealing.

"Why we can't take Greyhound?"

" 'Cause," Mama said, humoring her, "you can't get off a plane at fifty thousand feet up."

"Why we can't take a train down Souf? S'pose we gotta pee?"

" 'Cause," Mama said, "you can't accidentally miss the train at the rest stop. The rest stop is in the back of the plane."

"Mama, that don't even sound right," Gayle said. "Whoever heard of going to the bathroom in a plane? You could hit turbulence in mid-pee or something and mess up your clothes."

Mama told Gayle to stop acting simple, then reminded her to be where she was supposed to be when the plane landed. "Brother's not happy to begin with. You puttin' him out."

Gayle sank her face down upon her baby's soft hair. If only she could have gotten word to her girls last night. Gayle was sure Lynda Mama would take her and the baby in. Lynda Mama loved the baby. And why hadn't Troy shown up? He was probably at her house thinking he still gonna be a daddy. Too late now.

Gayle passed the time fantasizing. She made up scenes of last night with Troy at Mama's door yelling for her to come out . . . Junie acting up, with his wild self . . . Troy waxing the floor with Junie . . . Mama scared of Troy . . . Troy, Gayle, and José off to Troy Mama house . . . Troy schooling his mama on respecting Gayle . . . Troy Mama serving them pot roast, cabbage, and cornbread . . . Häagen-Dazs for dessert.

She came to in the airport, still jailed to Mama with José strapped to her belly. Mama didn't even try to be good company. As soon as the flight was called and the announcement was made for people with small children to board, Mama said "Come on" like there wasn't a moment to lose and ushered Gayle to the front of the line. She kissed José twice, then waved good-bye and hollered some final dos and don'ts for behaving down Souf.

Gayle didn't bother to turn around to hear any of that. She marched up the carpeted ramp and onto the plane, hoping to God Mama had gotten a good glimpse of her backside switching away. She followed a uniform-clad woman to her seat. A window seat.

"Unh-unh," Gayle cried. "I ain't sitting at no window."

A friendly but firm voice informed her it was the only seat available. The flight was booked solid.

Little kids excited about their first plane ride stuck their faces over their seats to gawk at her. Gayle could care less. She fussed and sucked her teeth until another flight attendant rushed to the scene.

"Miss, if you will be seated, perhaps we can persuade another passenger to trade," the other flight attendant suggested.

Gayle didn't trust her. She was too nice.

"We won't be able to do anything until the aisle is cleared."

Grudgingly, Gayle loosened the straps on the baby carrier and took her assigned seat. Mama think she so freakin' funny, she thought. Always gotta have the last laugh.

Twenty minutes passed without anyone faking an effort to find her a safer seat. The plane began to rumble. The same lying woman in uniform stood before her, grinning and explaining what to do with barf bags and emergency landing gear. The pilot got on the speaker to tell her she was going down Souf to live with strangers who didn't

21

want her in the first place. Then the plane started acting up, rumbling louder, turning, speeding down the asphalt.

Gayle peered timidly out of the window then jerked her head back. They were off the ground. A minute later she peeked again. "José! Look. There go that Freedom Lady and her torch. See! And those two giant buildings be on postcards. Look!"

José smiled up at her.

Unexpectedly the plane climbed straight up. Gayle crouched down, wrapped her arms around her baby, and squeezed her eyelids tight. When the plane appeared to be flying level she opened her eyes and looked out of the window. New York had gotten away from her. She and her baby were passing through clouds. It just wasn't right, passing through a cloud. Dead people passed through clouds on their way to heaven.

The baby didn't care for any of this plane travel and started crying. Gayle reached into her bag and pulled out a bottle to stick in his mouth. He still cried. Rocking him did not help. His cries progressed to screams. She could halfway tune him out if the nosy people crowding her with their looks would just leave her alone. Particularly the man on the aisle reading his paper. His heavy sighs, the constant folding and refolding of his paper, the head shaking, all directed at her. Didn't she know she and her son were a disgrace?

She glared at him. *Say something to me. I want you to . . .*

The woman seated between them turned to Gayle, offering fifty-year-old wisdom. "Babies' eardrums pop from the compression. It helps to have something for them to suck on."

"See this bottle in his mouth?" Gayle snapped. "So mind ya bizniz. Okay?"

The man with the newspaper glanced at the helpful woman. *What else could you expect from such a creature?*

Gayle didn't care. In fact she overcame her fear of looking out the window, preferring the clouds to the people.

"Is everything okay?" the flight attendant asked.

Gayle didn't want to be on no plane going Souf eating dry turkey sandwiches out of a cardboard box no ways. *Stomach still cramp from the abortion. Side still smarting from tussling with Mama. Back still sore from hauling the baby around. Cut off from Troy and the girls, being sold to slavery.*

"We fine," Gayle said, knowing the nice lady didn't want the real A to Z. "We fine."

But the flight attendant couldn't leave it alone. Compelled to put Gayle at ease, she complimented Gayle on taking good care of her baby brother. "Won't your mother be proud."

All she could say was "I'm sorry" when Gayle informed her she was the mother. She fled, spreading her niceness elsewhere. Gayle turned to the clouds.

❦ 4 ❦

FLOWERED ONES. Green ones. Paisley ones. Brown ones. A cello case. A birdcage. A footlocker. There. A plaid Woolworth suitcase and two A & P shopping bags joined by one of Junie's socks.

Ignoring what could only be looks of pity, Gayle stepped forward to gather her bags. She snickered, seeing those pitying glances dissolve to blindness as she struggled to the lounge area with her son, the shopping bags, and the suitcase. "All I need is to grow another hand," she muttered. She dropped down in the nearest cushioned lounge seat and tapped her foot, waiting to be claimed by people she didn't know.

Twenty minutes passed without anyone giving her and her child a thoughtful glance.

Maybe Uncle Luther forgot. Just as well. Then what? If they don't show in another fifteen minutes, call Mama collect, get her credit card number, jump back on a plane.

All Gayle knew about Mama's people was that Mama had left them and never looked back. Gayle assumed the parting had been mutual since no one from Columbus, Georgia, had ever come to New York to visit. Instead, an envelope bearing a Georgia postmark arrived every year without Christmas seals. The card always contained Bible

24

scripture and, at the bottom, **Pastor Luther Gates and Family** in boxy black lettering. There was no handwritten note that said "yawl come down." Might as well have been funeral cards.

Gayle wrapped "bankie" around José and rested her face next to his, which made her appear to be in hiding. She was. She rocked back and forth, praying Mama's family wouldn't show up. It was just after six. By nine or ten o'clock a cop would discover them sleeping in the airport and order them on the next plane to New York. José squirmed in her tight embrace and cried out from hunger and restlessness. "Don't worry," she whispered, as she reached in her shoulder bag for his bottle. "We'll be back home soon." José only cared about being fed.

"There she is! There she is!" A woman's voice carried across the terminal and brought Gayle out of hiding.

A big old skyscraping woman, a big-boned girl in kneesocks, and a tower of a man wearing a black suit and a joyless face came marching toward her.

That's them, Gayle thought. All giants like Mama. Junie s'posed to be filled out but he ain't exactly living right. Dog. Look at them. Aiming for the ceiling. They so big. Wonder what happened to me?

"Hello, Cousin Gayle," spilled the big-boned girl, her face swollen with gladness.

The man, Uncle Luther, didn't speak at first. He bent down, picked up the shopping bags and suitcase, then stated as though it caused him immense pain, "I'm your Uncle Luther. This is my wife, Virginia, our daughter, Constance."

She heard him perfectly, for his meaning rose above his creeping bellow. The skyscraping woman wasn't her aunt. The big-boned girl wasn't her cousin. They were *his* family. His.

So, the homies weren't really down, she noted, rising

25

from the lounge seat. Just as well, she told herself. The last thing she wanted was a bunch of strangers smothering her with hugs. What she couldn't forgive was their indifference toward José. No one tried to pinch his fat legs or twirl his curly hair. That was also just as well because she planned to snatch her baby back if they poured it on too thick and sugary.

With José close to her heart, Gayle followed the Gateses out to the parking lot, where the Georgia sun greeted her in all its abundance. Gayle gazed down to avoid the glare. The Gateses cast huge shadows on the gray asphalt. As if he felt her studying his shadow, Uncle Luther said, "It's a shame Ruth Bell spent money she didn't have sending you by airplane."

"No one asked her to." It slid out naturally. One of Mama's *don'ts*. Realizing the slip didn't stop her from jumping all in it. "I'd rather gone by train or bus or not at all. Nothing 'gainst yawl. I just as soon be home."

The aunt and the cousin, who held hands, gave each other a squeeze and a look of disbelief while they waited for something to happen.

Uncle Luther made a low, clicking sound like he was trying to lock his tongue deep in his throat. He swung around and dropped the bags.

"*What* did you say?" His nostrils flared, jaws tightened, the bellow now a roar. "What did you say?"

Too late to stop now, she decided. Besides, the sun was already beating her down. "I said—"

Uncle Luther's wife quickly stepped in, grabbing her niece by the arm. "Miss Gayle has had a long trip with no decent food, toting that baby a thousand miles. At least wait until she's home, settled, and fed before starting in." It was amazing. The woman's voice played. The angry man groaned, picked up the bags, and continued.

Constance offered Gayle a sympathetic look to soften

her up. Her sympathies fell flat against the surface of pure insolence and went sliding down fast. Constance dragged on behind her parents, hurt that her cousin refused her coded friendliness.

Gayle shot her a side glance and kept on walking.

How can I smile at you? Smiling means we know the same things, and you don't even know what I'm feeling. Cootie still sore from the abortion. Ears still ringing from the plane ride. Back fit to split wide open from playing the mule, but I'm s'posed to be grinning at you. . . . Ya big-boned-granny-stitched-up-white-sweater-pink-kneesock-wearing reject.

They settled into the car. Gayle stared out of the window to avoid the back of her uncle's head or her cousin's simple face.

Why couldn't they live in Atlanta, a city thumping and jumping? All them space-age buildings with glass elevators, statues, and malls. Manhattan probably didn't look this good.

The highway turned into a road that took them farther away from the city down into places buses didn't want to go. Miles of oak and pine lined both sides of the road, which was occasionally illuminated by DEER CROSSING signs and hunting regulations. Now, that's what they need in South Jamaica, Gayle mused. Bright yellow signs that screamed PLEASE DON'T SHOOT THE PEOPLE.

Coweta. Muscogee. Chattahoochee. Dog. They live in boonie country. Deep in the Georgia woods. Probably got a shack with an outhouse and a barn with chickens running around the front yard. I can see myself now, trooping ten miles to the well to fill the family water bucket. Shoulda conned my way back on the plane when I had the chance. No wonder Mama never found her way back home.

Gayle shivered. She could feel her cousin's stare. It was like the girl wanted to sniff her. Gayle closed her eyes and held José tighter.

Mama, wherever you are, I want you to hear what I'm

27

thinking: You ain't won yet. No way am I staying with these dead people down in the boonies.

After a half hour of no music, Uncle Luther making that throat-locking sound, feeling that big-boned cousin girl sniffing her out, and José's diaper full of doody, Uncle Luther's wife announced, "We're home."

Gayle opened her eyes. "Whoa," she moaned as they passed through a wooden gate. "Yawl live *here?*"

No one replied.

The house was old. Not old and falling apart, but grand and white with tall windows framed by black shutters, and white beams supporting its two-story porch. Like she was teaching ancient history, Uncle Luther's wife said that the house was modeled after some Italian architecture in the 1830s, then supplied particulars about the porches and windows and the gate they had passed through.

Gayle got out of the car with her baby.

They got land. Lots of it. Their own land like they know God personally—no wonder that man roars like some kinda king. Got the nerve to have trees upon trees with red-yellow peaches on 'em, other trees with huge white flowers—and they black. Black like my butt, living like this. Just look. Girls at home would die if they knew. And— Oh my God! Stones and crosses way over there. Dead people planted in the yard like rutabagas. Don't they have cemeteries in Georgia? They s'posed to! One good rain you got stiffs coming out the ground.

Constance noticed Gayle looking east toward the graveyard and offered to take her there. Acquaint her with the names of family members long gone.

"Not in this lifetime," Gayle cried, hurrying behind her aunt's flagging pleats.

A woman in a nurse's uniform greeted them at the door. She took Aunt Virginia by the hand and led her into another room. Uncle Luther left the bags in the parlor and retreated into a room that opened with two doors.

Constance picked up the bags. "I'll show you your room. Be careful with the baby coming up the stairs."

"Don't worry," Gayle said cupping José's head with her hand. "I got it."

"Him," Constance said. "You said 'it.' It's a him."

"That's what I said," Gayle fired back.

"No, Cousin Gayle," the girl insisted. "You called the baby 'it.' It's a him. Just a small point of grammar."

Gayle stopped right there. "Yo look, girlie. See this diaper full of doo-doo? I've been changing ones like it since day one. So don't be telling me about *him* and *it*. School's out. Okay?"

Now how do you like that? Got the nerve to be hurt when she the one started it.

Gayle followed her cousin upstairs. *Look at how she dresses. Kneesocks on a big girl like that. And that hairstyle. Straight out of* Mommy-Made-Me *magazine. And what kinda shoes are those?*

They entered a room where faded lilacs bloomed on the walls. Two long windows ushered in streams of sunlight. A mahogany crib stood next to an oversized mahogany bed. The dresser was nice, though Gayle didn't make too big a deal. People get excited when they think they've done something for you. Then they don't let you forget it.

"Hope you like the crib," Constance gushed like the grinning dummy Gayle knew she was. "It's the family crib, you know. I cleaned it since I was the last to have it."

"A new crib woulda been nice."

"But, Cousin, everybody used this crib. Auntie Ruth Bell, Daddy, me, Grandpa, Great-grandpa. It's about one hundred and twenty years old."

"Looks it," Gayle snapped. "Guess it'll do."

Constance chose to ignore Gayle's remark. "Thought

29

you'd like the quilt. Aunt Ruth Bell helped stitch it when she was a girl, but it's Great-grandmama's design."

"My mama don't go by no Ruth Bell. She goes by Ruby. And as for this quilt . . . what yawl got against buying a brand-new one?"

Gayle turned up her nose at all those patches. *Why couldn't they get a nice Disney quilt with Mickey Mouse or Donald Duck? Look at this old thing. All brown, beige, green, and ugly. Looks like something Mama made. No color.*

Gayle unharnessed José, who kicked her for the sheer joy of being freed. Constance stood by with an eager expression, wanting to help, but Gayle moved too fast. Besides, Constance looked like she didn't know the first thing about changing diapers.

"That's your name? Constance?" Gayle asked. "They don't call you that all day long, do they? Con-stan-suh. Hurts my throat."

Had she been true, homegirl would have said, "Like Gayle's so hot." Instead she sang cheerfully, "Everyone calls me Cookie," which was why Gayle couldn't like her.

"Big girl like you. How old you?"

"Sixteen," Cookie said, gazing at the baby. "He's just adorable."

"A real pain sometimes."

"Look at all of that curly hair. He should have been a girl."

"Don't think I didn't try for a girl," Gayle said with pride. "His wife had the girl and I had Stinkbutt. Ain't you stinky, baby?"

"His wife? Whose wife? The baby's father? He was married?"

"Yeah. So?" Gayle just knew it. Cookie was poised to correct the words out her mouth.

"Cousin Gayle, you're only fourteen. I thought some boy did this to you."

"Did what to me? What are you talking about?" Gayle asked calmly.

"Didn't he force you or trick you?" Cookie asked.

Gayle laughed so hard she had to swallow. "Cookie, how old are you again?"

Cookie said sixteen.

Gayle just shook her head and picked up the baby. Not only was Cookie big-boned like Mama and dressed for a schoolyard beating, but she was family and a reject. The girls at home would just die. The abortion, the plane ride, and now Cookie.

❧5❧

"Daddy needs his peace and quiet," Cookie said, leading Gayle and José down the winding steps. She pointed to the closed double doors. "That's his sanctuary. Where he goes to reflect on his sermons."

Not fooled for a minute, Gayle coughed up a muffled laugh. The only thing Uncle Luther was reflecting on was the total sum Gayle and her baby were costing him in money and embarrassment.

José clung to his mother, gumming her neck. "Stop!" Gayle scolded, though he continued. "I hate it when he does that."

She took in the whole downstairs, which included a parlor, Uncle Luther's study, the kitchen, and an enclosed dining room, which Cookie said was used for entertaining only. Cookie pointed and noted like a wind-up tour guide: "See this clock, Cousin Gayle? You would be interested to know . . ." What Gayle knew was that this was hardly a place to feel at home in. It was a place with history mounted on the walls and furniture not meant to be disturbed by actual use.

"Yawl got too much house," Gayle complained. "How many people live here anyway?"

"Just us. Mommy. Daddy. Me. Great. Just us."

"Great. Who that?"

"Great-grandmama. You'll meet her when we bring up her supper."

"She don't come down to eat?"

"Oh, no," Cookie said, amazed that Gayle didn't know better. "Great stays in bed. She's going to her reward soon."

"Reward?"

"Great's ready to die," Cookie announced cheerfully. "Definitely before summer's out."

"What? Well why ain't she in the hospital where she belong?"

Gayle's outburst left Cookie momentarily bewildered until she recalled her daddy saying most New Yorkers didn't know old age. They died horrible young deaths that would forever lock them out of paradise. Why anyone—meaning Aunt Ruth Bell—would want to live and die in New York was beyond his understanding.

They went into the kitchen, which Gayle found spacious and ridiculously well stocked like something straight out of Mama's *Better Homes and Gardens* magazines, with copper pots and utensils hanging from above, a butcher-block-topped island sitting in the midst of black and white tiles, real brick walls, and varnished wood cabinets. Mama would go crazy in a big old kitchen like this instead of that turn-stove-turn-sink-turn-fridge back home. Mama was a cooking fool.

"Come and see the pantry," Cookie said, opening a door within the kitchen. Gayle cradled her baby protectively and poked her head in. The pantry back home was a closet, and she wasn't letting that cousin girl push her into no dark closet. Cookie just didn't strike Gayle as being all there. She was too quick to be hurt or happy about nothing.

Gayle stepped inside. Two washing machines stood side

33

by side. A huge freezer, which Cookie hefted open, was filled with meat in leg, rack, and shoulder portions—not no $3.99 fool-sized cuts wrapped in cellophane and Styrofoam. The pantry shelves were lined with mason jars and canned goods, and a whole shelf was dedicated to seasonings packed in pint-sized tin boxes. Twenty-pound sacks of rice, white potatoes, sweet potatoes, flour, sugar, salt, and charcoal stood along the wall like squat, fat men.

No wonder these people bigger than Jack's giant. They probably load one whole sack of sweet potatoes on they plates for supper.

"This was Aunt Ruth Bell's favorite place," Cookie said. "I know she told you how she liked to hide in the pantry and concoct all kinds of wildness."

Gayle snorted. Whatever interest she had had in the pantry ended right there. "Listen. Just 'cause you and yo mama hold hands don't mean me and Mama act like that, so don't go making pictures of me and Mama baking cobblers on Sunday."

Cookie led Gayle and José back to the kitchen where they could sit and talk. Aunt Virginia came into the kitchen after seeing the nurse to her car. She asked her niece how she liked her room, though it wasn't a sincere inquiry. Before Gayle could flit her eyelids and complain about that tacky old lilac wallpaper, the hundred-year-old furniture, the drab baby quilt, and the absence of a television set in her room, her aunt said, "It was your mama's room when she was coming up. Ruth Bell and I have been best friends since Sunday school. Couldn't pry us apart. We were like sisters. Many a day was spent in that room plotting and carrying on."

Gayle gave her aunt a washed-down version of the looks she had been giving Cookie. "Sorry, Miss Aunt Virginia, I can't picture that. You and Mama."

"Auntie," the woman said, trying it out herself. "Auntie will do. Now, how's your mother, sweetie? Is she all right?"

"I guess."

"And Junior? Ruthie used to send me all of Junior's pictures and newspaper clippings, though legs like those don't belong in basketball shorts. Ruthie was so proud of him."

Gayle smirked. Let Miss Auntie fill in the blanks. Served Mama right for playing up Junie and not having nothing nice to say about Gayle. If Miss Auntie could see Junie all thin and glassy-eyed on the sofa she'd know what kinda mama Mama was and what kinda son Junie was.

"And how are you, sweetie?" Miss Auntie whispered as if she didn't want Cookie to hear—which was stupid because Cookie was sitting right there with ears the size of Dumbo's. "Do you need anything, sweetie?"

Gayle repressed a smirk, thinking, Miss Auntie, you ain't slick and I ain't stupid. You just wanna know about the abortion. Do I need anything? How about a one-way bus ticket to South Jamaica, New York.

To her aunt, she crooked her neck girl-like and said, "I needs a stroller to get around. But I'm okay. Nothing hurts."

"You'll find a few things in your top drawer just in case," Miss Auntie said tenderly, setting aside Gayle's saucy looks, her teeth sucking, her transparent, muffled laughs.

Cookie's chair scooted in closer. It was like Cookie wanted to sniff out the mystery her mother sang around in cautious, soothing tones.

Gayle cut eyes at her cousin, catching her in the act. Cookie seemed to retract in shame.

Reject

35

"I know Ruth Bell spoke to you before putting you on the plane. I'm sure she told you what we will and will not have in our house."

"Yeah, awright," Gayle said. "Go on. Hit me with it."

Miss Auntie raised an eyebrow. The phrase *hit me* was set aside, but noted.

"Everyone has a job," her aunt began. "Yours will be helping with the housework and caring for Great when Cookie is out. We are always in motion—be it for school, work, the church, or the community. We're always moving and doing. Cookie has youth fellowship and choir practice, and she volunteers at the soup kitchen. During the school year she's even busier."

Gayle shot Cookie a glance. *Don't go blushing. Look at you.*

"Things must get done around the house."

"Seems like yawl been managing all this time without me."

"And now we'll manage a little better," her aunt rejoined, hot on the tail of Gayle's remark. "Understand me, sweetie. I love your mother like a sister, but these are the only terms on which your uncle will have you here— kept busy. You see, we don't have the kind of goings on you're used to. We're a family. Everyone's actions impact on everyone else."

Gayle knew that *impact* word. It meant to hit hard. She half-smiled, rolled her eyes to the ceiling, and thought, I'm shaking.

"If you decide to go to school come fall, you'll make baby-sitting arrangements with someone in the church. Cookie will take you around."

"Whatchoo mean *if* I decide? I don't have to go to school? You not making me?"

"That's your choice."

Gayle caught Cookie's face agog with disbelief.

Miss Auntie caroled just as nicely, "You have enough education in your lap. If you don't want to be bothered with school, no sense sending you out there for trouble."

"Oh, snap! I can't wait to tell Mama I ain't going to school. She'll flip. She's always on me for schooling and doing homework and being somebody."

"Why, Miss Gayle, you are somebody. You're Emanuel's mother. As for homework, you'll have plenty, so you need not concern yourself about school if you are not inclined."

Gayle mimicked silently, If you are not inclined, loving the haughtiness that was so "Miss Auntie."

"Mama!" Cookie blurted out.

Miss Auntie held her hand up flat and lowered her head, meaning "Hush, child." "Your free time must be spent productively. We will not have any hanging about town—that is, if you find your way into town.

"Dinner is our time for togetherness. We do not bring friction to the table and there is no back talk here. I won't always be able to jump between you and your uncle Luther if you're foolish enough to try him.

"I'm not expecting you to be involved in trouble of any kind. This is not that kind of house, Miss Gayle. And furthermore, I don't expect any boys to know more than your name, who your people are, and where you live.

"Now, being Ruth Bell's girl, I suspect you can cook, so you will help out in the kitchen and with the laundry. If any of this is not agreeable, speak up now."

"Yawl wanna work me to death, see that I have no fun."

"You won't be doing any more than anyone else here. We all work around the house. And on Sundays, we come

37

together with our congregation to worship and share in the spirit of the Lord."

"That's not what I'm talking about. I need some fun. Fun. You know, fun. Who gon' watch the baby when I go out?"

Her aunt smiled. "Why, Miss Gayle, he is your little bundle of fun. You will take him with you."

José took his cue and squealed in his mother's ear.

"I think it stinks," she wailed, then stuck the pacifier in his mouth. "I don't wanna stay here."

"Call your mother and tell her so. But know this before you start dialing: She's not laying out any money for your return. Now if you wish to earn your way back, that's your choice. Like every choice in life, it will cost you."

"I'll hitch."

Miss Auntie smiled again, the smile that told Gayle the ammo was ready. "Why, Miss Gayle, don't you know what happens to young ladies caught hitching with their babies?"

Cookie came this close to asking "What?"

Gayle had an idea and decided to spare herself the lecture about being stopped by the police, branded an unfit mother, having her baby ripped from her arms, and being thrown in the pokey with hard women.

"Okay," Gayle said. "What about social services?"

"Excuse me, sweetie?"

Miss Auntie was just being cute. She had that smile on her face. This was worse than being stomped on by Mama. Mama she could try to hit back.

"All I need is to go down to welfare. I can save from my monthly allotment and earn my ticket that way."

Miss Auntie gave Gayle a pitying look. "Sweetie, welfare isn't a way of life," she said softly. "Welfare is for poor souls who have no way and no family. You have an abundance of family, love, and support."

"Oh yeah. I'm still hurting from all that love and support Uncle Luther gave me at the airport."

Miss Auntie couldn't refute it. The child was half-raised and ignorant, but not stupid. "Your uncle will come around" is all that she offered.

"It's not fair. I didn't do nothing to no one, and yawl treat me like a slave and a criminal. On top of it, I'm s'posed to praise the Lord for being stuck here."

"Cousin, don't cry," Cookie said. "You know we love you."

"Cry? Me? Do I look like I'm crying? I just want out."

"All right, all right," Miss Auntie said. "I'm sorry you feel this way, but you'll come around. This is our home, not a place of punishment. In time we'll grow into each other. We're family. Family. Now, we've had a long day and we're all starving. Let's set the table."

"You can use the strainer to make the baby's food," Cookie offered. "It's in this drawer."

Gayle glared at Cookie. *I was not crying. I don't cry.*

Miss Auntie stretched out her arms until Gayle lifted José toward her. She took him and smiled, appreciating Gayle's inability to just hand over her baby.

"Isn't it great having a baby in the house?" Cookie gushed.

Miss Auntie held him up and said in a far-off way, "This house could use some life," like she was talking to herself.

Gayle sat with empty arms, rolling her eyes while the two went on crediting family members she never heard of for her baby's eyes, his puffy cheeks, his coloring, his determination. It was like she had had nothing to do with it at all.

"T<small>RAY'S READY</small>," Cookie said. "You'll just love Great, and she's anxious to meet you and the baby. We haven't had a baby in the house since me."

With José heavy and sleepy in her arms from creamed chicken and sweet potatoes, Gayle followed her cousin up the stairs. She counted twenty-eight steps and rested on the top step. "Whew!" she cried, rubbing the small of her back. "Why yawl need all these rooms? This house is too big."

"It was a plantation," Cookie said.

"Oh yeah? What yawl plant besides dead people in the front yard?"

"Cousin Gayle, you are just too much." Cookie laughed. "I know you've had the Civil War and slavery in school."

"I know about slavery, all right," she said. "I'm the house slave, remember? That is, till I break free."

"Cousin, you are too funny for words. Too funny."

"Hee haw."

Cookie pushed open the door to Great's room with her shoulder. She peered in then whispered, "She's sleeping. C'mon in."

Gayle tiptoed up to the door and looked inside before

entering. She held José so tight he squirmed and patted her face. The thought of being with a person who could stiffen and die at any moment horrified and disgusted her. She went in expecting to smell and see death.

There was a faint mixture of lilac and disinfectant in the air. Everything in the room was old-fashioned—or as Miss Auntie would say, "authentic." The furniture, the yellowed crocheted doilies, the wallpaper. Old. The woman lying in the bed was so old she ran out of age. She wasn't so much wrinkly as her once bright skin cast ginger shadows along her fallen cheeks. Her long white hair was braided up like a child's in too many plaits. Cookie must have done that, Gayle surmised. It looked like the sort of thing only Cookie would think of.

"Great. Great. You sleep?"

Her great-grandmother's eyes were still shut and her face placid when she responded, "You mean Great, you dead?"

"Well?" Cookie teased.

"Stop yo' fooling," she said, pausing between each word. Then her eyes opened and went straight to Gayle. "Who that?"

Cookie meant to bring Gayle forward but ended up pushing her, as Gayle seemed stuck to the floor.

"Ruthie," the woman said. "Come here, baby."

"Great-grandmama, that's not Ruth Bell. That's her daughter, Gayle Ann Whitaker, and this is her baby boy, Emanuel."

Gayle recoiled at her name said long and correctly instead of simply "Gayo" with the l silent. She gave Cookie an evil look, letting her know she didn't appreciate that "Emanuel" thing.

Great propped herself up with some effort and strained to see the baby. "Luther," she called out.

"Daddy downstairs. This is Gayle Ann's baby, Emanuel," Cookie said. She whispered to Gayle, "Great forgets sometimes, or her mind's in the past. Don't take it personally if she never gets to know you."

"Trust me, I won't," Gayle said. "And his first name is José, not Emanuel."

"Oh, I know 'bout you. You the one like to taste the breeze high up 'cross the crease your backside. D'ain nothing new. Come here so I can see you."

Cookie's eyes bugged out. Slack jawed, Gayle stood unaffected until the picture hit her all at once. Her face tightened. That faded prune said she knew about Gayle throwing her booty up in the air for Tom, Dick, and Harry.

"Yo, look, Granny—"

"Daddy preached a powerful sermon this morning!" Cookie jumped in. "Sister Taylor fell out! But you know Sister Taylor . . ." Cookie started spooning Great creamed sweet potatoes, wiping beneath her lip like she would a baby.

Great wouldn't leave well enough alone. She kept staring at Gayle's face hard with eyes that sang, "Oh yeah, I know about you."

Gayle tapped her foot and shifted José's weight, thinking, She lucky she old and she family. You can't be jumping in someone's face throwing out their business like that.

"Doesn't the baby favor Grandpa's baby picture?" Cookie said to Gayle. "Grandpa was Great's son. Go look. Right up on the bureau."

Gayle dragged her feet to the bureau to see the resemblance, but also to avoid the woman's eyes. "Which one?" Gayle asked. "They all got the same face."

"Um-hm," Great agreed. "All them Luthers."

"Now, look at Daddy's baby picture. He and José could be twins."

"Don't wish that face on my child," Gayle cried. "Your daddy's one evil-looking man."

"Daddy evil looking?"

"Could scare the bark off a tree," Great said.

"Right!" Gayle signified. That old woman snatched it clean off her tongue.

Cookie stuck another spoonful in Great's mouth, wiped around her chin, and gave her water.

Great gulped the water hard. "Sure would like a taste before I die."

"Great, you know Daddy don't allow no spirits in the house," Cookie said.

"Not spirits," Great said. "Just the old family recipe."

"Old family liquor," Cookie said, like she was correcting a child. "Drink this water. It's good for you."

Great made a face only Gayle could appreciate. *The woman they said was going to glory wasn't going no time soon. She still had life in her. They were just killing her, doing her like a child and boring her to death. No wonder she snappy and full of nerve. All she want is a sip of her old family recipe.*

Sure enough. Cookie ran her mouth about church things and neighbors and the weather until Great's lids gave out. They left the room as quietly as they had entered. Gayle put José in the wooden box they called a crib and laid the drab quilt over him. They sat on the bed that had belonged to Mama.

"I don't see what the big deal is. She gonna die soon anyway. Might as well give her what she wants."

"Let her meet Jesus with peach liquor on her breath?"

"Meet Jesus? Cookie, be serious." Gayle laughed.

Cookie was genuinely mortified.

"Cousin Gayle, don't you *want* to be saved?"

"Hell, no," Gayle declared. "Save what? We living to be living. Not to be saving."

43

"Cousin, you wouldn't say that if you heard Daddy preach salvation. Daddy can preach."

"Puh-leez. I can't even stay awake in church Christmas and Easter. Only days I go. But you know, José was the best-dressed baby in church on Easter. Yup."

"Cousin, you'll love church here. Daddy is so inspiring. I couldn't wait to be saved after hearing one of Daddy's sermons on salvation, but Daddy and Mama made me wait until I was fourteen. They said, 'Be a child while you are a child. Once you take salvation you're responsible for your rights and wrongs.' Well, my fourteenth birthday fell on a Sunday, so you know what I wished for."

Uncle Luther wasn't the only preacher in the family. Cookie was going for some hallelujahs. Could she get a witness?

"I'da held out for a gift," Gayle said.

"You know, Cousin, salvation is the greatest gift of all. There's nothing like it on this earth. Your body just surrenders to the spirit. Some people fall out. I couldn't stop crying when I got saved. I was so happy."

"You cried," Gayle deadpanned.

"Everybody cries."

"Not me."

"What about when you had the baby?"

"Not one tear."

"It must have hurt like nothing you ever felt before. I know you cried."

They folded their legs. Cookie was pitched forward, angled for listening. Gayle fixed for telling. This was what she was missing. Entertaining her girls with her stories. And they'd "yup," "right," and "um-hm" in all the right places.

"I heard they put the young ones to sleep," she began. "But the nurse—a rusty old black one—said, 'Nothing for this one. She can take it.' I told her, 'Nurse, I'm young. I'm not s'posed to feel no pain.' She gave me a dirty look like I disgusted her and said I shoulda thought about that while I was spreading my legs. Mama couldn't take off from work early and I didn't have no doctor so I straightened her out myself. Still wouldn't give me no knockout. Called it teaching me a lesson. Oh, I hate it when people try to correct my world all in one shot. Honey, I gets evil then. You shoulda heard her chewing me out, expecting me to break down and cry and say I'm sorry for being pregnant. So I laughed in her face. Yup. And those pains were shooting up my back. But see if I cried.

"Oh! That ain't even the funny part," Gayle went on, spurred by Cookie's interest. "There was this old broad in the bed next to me. About thirty, having her *first* baby. Talk about crying! Her husband's holding her hand saying, 'Breathe, honey. You can do it.' Honest to God, they was cracking me up. Black people—acting all simple. Then we was in the same room after the delivery. That old broad cried every three minutes. Cried when they brought the baby in, cried when they took it away. She even cried after counting his fingers and toes. So I asked her, 'Why you crying all the time?' She said—straight up, no lie—'Life is beautiful,' and started crying again." Having delivered her punch line, Gayle broke into convulsive laughter.

Cookie pictured her cousin on the burning coals of hell. "Didn't you cry .   when you had that   · when Auntie Ruth Bell made you .. "

"Oh, that 'bortion?" Gayle shot out plainly. "What? Me cry so Mama could start hollering 'What you crying for?' Please. You ain't been speeched until Mama speeches you dry. Believe me, if I have a choice between a speeching and a beating I'll take a pop upside the head anytime."

"Cousin, between you and me, I don't think Aunt

Ruth Bell should have put your souls in jeopardy like that."

"Well," Gayle said, her exuberance winding down, "I didn't cry then. No use starting up now."

"Don't you feel like some part of you is missing?"

"Like what?" Gayle asked. The only missing part was what the doctors took out and wouldn't let her see.

Cookie couldn't explain about the missing thing but insisted, "You must want to cry. If I went through all you went through I'd be in tears."

"Goodness, Cookie. Get a hold of yourself. I'm still ticking and kicking. Don't get yourself all worked up. Jeez."

Cookie was embarrassed, while her cousin seemed to have no feelings. She got up to leave, saying, "It's late. I'll wake you in the morning to do Great."

Gayle pushed the baby's crib closer to her bed. He didn't seem to care that he was in an old wooden box a thousand miles from home. He had passed out from all of that food Miss Auntie had pushed down his throat. And who was gonna have to stay up and rub his belly when he started hollering all night? Not Miss Auntie and certainly not Mama who was at home having the last laugh while Gayle was stuck in a room with no TV and no music and no life 'cept José in a house full of Holy Rollers.

Gayle looked down at her son. "Least you could do is cry," she whispered, although it was clear from his peaceful face that he was happy.

7

I<small>F THAT</small> big-boned cousin girl said how natural Gayle was at caring for Great one more time she'd slap the fat off her. Cookie ain't slick, Gayle thought. She just glad she don't have to do the cleaning, changing, and feeding. Look at how fast she cut out to do her volunteer work.

"It ain't fair," Gayle muttered. "Why I gotta be the slave?"

She left Great, determined to do something for herself, just because she felt like it. Gayle lifted her son out of the crib, bathed and dressed him, then announced, "We going out to play." She took a spoon and two jars of strained fruit from her shoulder bag in spite of what Miss Auntie had said about jarred baby food. No way was she making extra work for herself, throwing fresh bananas in a blender. Not when Miss Gerber done picked 'em, peeled 'em, mashed 'em, and put 'em in nice little jars.

Gayle placed her son on her hip and marched downstairs and out into the backyard. Beckoning arms of fragrant peach trees called them to enjoy the shade. She chose a tree full of yellow fruit to sit under. It was a good spot. The house blocked the view of the eastern side of the property, where crosses and headstones seemed to have grown yet another inch out of the red earth.

She looked down at her son. "You likes it here, don't you?"

He laughed at her. His mama was the funniest thing, especially the way her eyes got bigger when her mouth made singsong.

"I hates it," Gayle snapped. "It's too hot and ain't nothing to do. Don't hear no cars, no music on the street, no street period! It's dead 'round here. Just dead. Even got dead folks planted in the yard."

He drooled and cooed, listening to her voice ride up and down while her hands stabbed into the air. He caught hold of a finger and tried to bite it.

"Stop dat! Just stop dat!" she scolded, though her chuckle gave her away.

A long shadow on the porch told her to look up. Uncle Luther imposed his height and girth in the frame of the screen door, cutting off the light that flowed through it. Unlike Cookie and Miss Auntie, Uncle Luther didn't bother with "good morning." Instead he bellowed, "Grandma needs cleaning," then stepped away, allowing light to pass through the screen.

Gayle squinted and spit out curses at her uncle, who by now was in his study.

"Is my name Fifi? Run, Fifi. Jump, Fifi. Go clean, Fifi. He must think I'm a dog, snapping his fingers at me. S'pose I wanna play with my baby?"

José reached for her finger and tried to bite it again.

"Stop dat!" she yelled.

He let out a scream.

"Hush that noise 'fore I pop you!" She scooped him up and brought him inside the house. José only cried louder, his face reddening. "I mean it," she said raising both her hand and voice.

How did they expect her to watch José and do for Miss Great at the same time? How? Just how? She couldn't leave José alone but she couldn't take him in there. He might roll off the bed or swallow who knows what if she turned her back. She couldn't make a move without thinking about him, him, him. And even if she could go somewhere he'd be strapped to her. Dog! Everyone was snatching her freedom right from under her feet.

Gayle kicked her door open, when she could have just as easily turned the knob. She put José in his crib. He let out a holler, both hands reaching up to her. She ran out of the room and closed the door to keep from smacking him.

Why he gotta need me like that?

She went into the bathroom to fill the porcelain washbasin. The running tap water cooled her hands. When she felt herself calming, Gayle dried her hands and carried the basin into Great's room.

She could smell right away that Miss Great needed changing when she entered the room. Miss Great was stiff looking. Maybe even dead. Last thing she wanted to do was clean a dead person.

"Miss Great. Miss Great," she whispered, praying the old woman was only sleeping.

Great's eyes popped open, which Gayle felt she did on purpose. All the same, Gayle sighed, relieved. The last thing she wanted was to be the one who found her dead.

"Miss Great, I come to clean you."

Gayle remembered everything Cookie had shown her. 'Sides, wasn't much different than doing for José. She

49

removed the soiled padding from Miss Great and began wiping and sponging. Mess like a baby, Gayle thought, putting on fresh padding. Unlike Cookie, who manhandled Great clumsily, Gayle took her time changing Great's cotton gown. Miss Great was real easy and didn't fight against her movements like José.

"Miss Great, don't you miss going outside?" Gayle asked. "It feel like prison in here."

"Miss a lot of things," she said.

"Like that peach liquor you wanted Cookie to get."

"Freshie, that ain't liquor. More like a tea. A healing tea."

"Anything you say, Granny."

Great pursed her lips like she had to spit. "Something ugly as you otta be sweet."

Gayle chuckled. As many boys told her she was a fine yella honey, she knew better. And Troy was gonna buy a gold tooth to cap her chipped one. Man, she had to get back to South Jamaica!

Great studied Gayle's face then shook her head. "A boy draws on his mama's looks. And you ugly—mercy, mercy! Ain't seen nothing so ugly."

"Granny, is you trying to break on me?" Gayle said.

"Just look at you. All your teef fell out."

"Just got one chipped toof," Gayle said.

"Chirrens rob your teef and more. Every child a toof will drop."

"That's just an old wise tale."

"Don't I know it," Great testified. "Better get this wisdom while I got it to give. It's handed down like the recipe."

Gayle rolled her eyes and thought, She a hustler. An old hustler. Face suddenly full of color like she gonna live another year.

"Old Luther's mammy used to make it," Great continued. "Passed it on to me. Got it from her mammy, and so on back to the root. Know how t'tell a groom in love? He'll walk miles and miles to fill his jar with the healing. Know how t'tell a old married man? Missus come miles and miles fill her own jar." Great laughed, straining her. Gayle didn't get the joke but said "hah hah" to be polite.

"Mothers brought daughters for cramps. Womens took it for headaches, backaches, and all women pains. Good for the change too."

Gayle knew about cramps and backaches. She didn't know about changing, though Great looked like she done changed a couple of times. She so old.

"I suspect you can use some family recipe, being all through it. A little taste will put things right."

"Miss Great, you ain't slick. You just want some liquor and you want me to get it."

"Listen, you toofless yella frog."

"Fa-rog?"

"I was nothing but fourteen when I slipped my first. Slipped another one three months after that. Mammy Gates knew what to do. How to make everything heal. I got my strength up and had a giant. My Sonny. Carried him full time. Now, seem like you could use a healing. Make that recipe and you'll be whole in no time."

"I ain't miscarried," Gayle declared. "I had an abortion."

"Keep pulling on them roots. See if nothing grows."

"Nothing wrong with me," Gayle insisted.

"Nothing the recipe can't heal."

Make, make, make. Great was asking her to *do* another thing. "Why don't Cookie go buy you some?"

"Can't buy family recipe. Got to be *made*," Great said. "Cookie is her daddy's baby. He put it in her head it's wicked. What I calls healing, he calls hoodoo. Devil rooting."

"Oh, it's some kind of crime against God? Cookie big on God."

"Little Luther hides 'hind God," Great whispered, as if Luther could hear them. "You'd never know his daddy was a big drinking man. Not that Sonny was no drunk. He was a giant. Laughed big, talked big, drank big. Y'always knew when Sonny home. He made the house come alive.

"Sonny was a marching preacher, now. Got kilt during them Civil Rights marches. When Little Luther went to get the body all he could remember about his daddy was the smell of bourbon. Little Luther never forgot it, never forgave it. When he got to be grown, took over his daddy's church, Little Luther made spirits his number-one devil for destroying mens and families. Ain't been no one making family recipe since Ruthie. We made it in secret, you know."

"Now you want me to make it?"

"If I could get up in them trees and pick them peaches myself I wouldn't sorrow you with the recipe."

"Me climb a tree? Granny, you *must* be mad."

"Ain't you never climbed a tree? Played Indian or something? What kinda gal is you?"

"Kids don't be climbing trees in South Jamaica," Gayle said.

"You don't want the ones up in the trees no way. You want the ripe ones already dropped. Ripe, not spoilt."

"What I know 'bout cooking up wine?"

"Best get this wisdom while I got it. I'mo pass it down like Mammy Gates passed it on to me."

Great's eyelids fluttered, heavy with fatigue. Her lips moved soundlessly.

Gayle leaned forward to hear better. "What's that, Miss Great? What?"

"Cut them up. Tho' in the pit. Won't need much water, not more'n y'otta. Go round to Mahalia. She won't fail you."

"Who that?"

"Tree 'longside the peach. Mahalia got cramp bark. If Little Luther cut that down—like he always threatened to do—d'ain nothing. Snatch you some catnip. Batch growing near the headstones."

"Over by the dead people?" Gayle was mortified.

"If none of that, squaw vine do fine."

"They sell it at the store?"

"Shave off a bit black licorice. Tho' it all in the jar 'long with the peaches. Set cotton cloth over it and let it keep in the dark. Some mason jars in the pantry. I think that little girl uses them to plant things in," she whispered.

"What little girl?" Gayle asked.

"Little girl what runs 'hind Little Luther giggling and grinning. It's a wonder he could stand something that silly."

"Cookie?"

Great made that bout-to-spit face. "Ginny."

Gayle almost asked who Ginny was when she realized Great was in the past remembering Aunt Virginia as a young girl.

"Don't let Little Luther find it," Great said before her eyes closed from exhaustion. "He's looking for the devil."

"Unh-unh."

Gayle left Great and returned to her room, determined

53

to take José back outside to play. She looked into the crib. José had worn himself out crying and was sleeping on his belly. She turned his head more to the side and stroked his hair. She wanted to do something so he wouldn't have nightmares of her during his nap. She wanted to sing a lullaby, though none came to mind. Instead, she sang over and over, "Go round to Mahalia, she won't fail you" and anything else she could remember from the recipe.

❦ 8 ❦

"I KNEW something was up," Gayle told José, who gazed up at her from the blanket he sat on. "Reason Miss Auntie only wrote *laundry* on my list last night was she knew laundry was an all-day affair."

José banged on the rubber basket with both hands.

"It's like she knew I planned to get into some trouble. Get those ingredients. Brew up some recipe. Great'll have to wait another day."

She jumped up to pull the line down in order to pin linen napkins to the clothesline. *Why couldn't they have a dryer? They had two washers plus all the money in the world. What was the problem?*

"And miss all this sunlight?" Miss Auntie had said the night before. Work, slave, work, is what she meant.

Gayle was no stranger to laundry duty. She had always washed two or three loads for Mama on Saturdays, but never no jailhouse loads like what Miss Auntie had in mind. She almost cracked a rib stretching to pin the clothes to a line that was obviously built for skyward women like Miss Auntie and Cookie. José's bibs and T-shirts were the hardest to hang, as they didn't drape. Not to mention Cookie's big old cotton bloomers and

55

those kneesocks. And Miss Auntie had a thing for linen napkins. Miss Auntie said paper napkins were bad for the environment. Bad for the environment, nothing. Miss Auntie used linen napkins at dinner to be showing out. Then there was Great's things. Gayle could use an entire line to hang Miss Great's sheets and bedgowns, which she went through like Kleenex. At least Miss Auntie brought Uncle Luther's shirts to the cleaners. Gayle didn't want to do any more for her uncle than she had to.

A gnat hung at her ear, needling her lobe. She swatted furiously. *Damn gnats. They were everywhere. Swat one, here come his brother. Take care of him, here come his cousins.*

What was Cookie doing that she couldn't come out and help with this laundry? Didn't they say at the clinic no heavy housework for six weeks? She smiled, thinking, Miss Auntie would make her lie down if she said she had the woman pains. She laughed aloud. José laughed with her. Woman pains wouldn't cut no cloth with Mama, 'cause Mama'd say, "You got to be a woman to have woman pains." Gayle told José, "That Mama be pissing me off and making me laugh."

The laundry basket was empty again. She pulled it away from José and started for the pantry. José cried out. She was leaving him.

"What you spec me to do? I can't carry you and get clothes too. Stay there," she yelled back.

José wailed.

Gayle refused to turn around. All of that cooing and coddling would only slow her down. She went into the pantry, where two washing machines were filled with whites. One machine completed the spin cycle while the other was churning strong. José's cries were not to be drowned out by the washers. She moved quickly, emptying a damp pile into her basket. She ran outside with her basket to her son, whose arms were outstretched.

"See! Ain't nothing to be crying about." She wiped his face. "You hungry, ain't you?"

"Aaak!"

"Awright, awright," she said, setting the basket on the grass. "I kinda figured that one little jar wouldn't hold you." She took out a jar of cereal and a spoon from her apron. She sat down, unscrewed the jar, and began to feed him. He fussed, knocking the spoon away. "Had some real food, don't want no jar food no more. Well you gon' starve, li'l man. I'm not creaming no sweet potatoes and grits 'cause you getting spoiled eating these people food."

José blew spit bubbles at his mama.

"Eat this or eat nothing."

José reached, trying to knock the spoon away. He shook his head left then right and blew more spit bubbles.

"Ain't got all day. Stop being stupid and eat this."

The screen door swung open. Miss Auntie came flying out of the house like the roof was on fire.

"Did I hear right? Did you call this sweet little angel stupid? We don't allow such a word in our house, let alone on a baby. He'll grow up stupid because you told him he was stupid."

Gayle glared at her aunt. "Okay," she said. "Eat this here cereal or starve, little genius."

Her aunt did not care for the remark and snatched up the baby. "Emanuel, sweetheart," she said, knowing full well his name was José, "you hungry, baby?" He stopped fussing the minute she opened her mouth. "Auntie will feed you."

Gayle folded her arms and squinted at Auntie, who paid her no mind. Not only had Miss Auntie undone her mothering, but she had managed to soothe her baby with her lilting voice. Gayle watched her son drool at the sight of Miss Auntie's mouth oozing honey as though that were food enough. And when Miss Auntie carried him off, he didn't cry or search for her over Miss Auntie's shoulder.

A gnat landed on Gayle's arm. She smacked it hard. Had to smack something even if it was her own skin.

"See if I care."

She yanked a towel out of the basket and threw it up to the line. A pain, sharp like a hand squeezing her deep down inside, made her double over. She stayed bent, waiting for the grip on her insides to ease. It was the woman pains! They were for real. Better not fool around, she thought. She sat in the grass and rocked back and forth on her sits bones to pass the pain. The sun was in her eyes when she could stand on her feet. A tree with the widest trunk stretched out its arms, then tilted its leafy head upward from a sudden breeze. It had to be Mahalia. The only fruitless tree standing next to the peach trees.

She had to make that peach recipe. It would put her right, like Great said. She took a few baby steps toward the tree. She stopped, hearing the back door swing open. It was Cookie.

" 'Bout time you got out here. What was you doing besides eating breakfast?"

"For your information, Cousin Gayle, I had the bathrooms to clean, all the floors to mop, and the carpets to vacuum. Then I gave Great her wash-off, fed her breakfast, and read her Psalms."

"Yeah, yeah. So you busy." Gayle's breath was heavy.

"Cousin, are you all right?"

"It ain't nothing. Just a cramp."

"Why didn't you use the stool? Look at you. You're a midget."

"Who you calling midget?" Gayle asked sharply. "Do you hear me calling you out?—though I could."

Cookie had no intention of paying back ugly. She went into the pantry.

Gayle took a few deep breaths. She rubbed her pelvis and looked to the tree. Mahalia. The pains seemed to pass.

Cookie returned with the stool. "Mama's in there feeding José," she said cheerfully. "She loves him terribly."

"If she loves babies so much why'd she stop at you?"

Cookie spoke secretively. "Great said Mama almost died having me and couldn't have no more babies."

"Those the breaks," Gayle sang, puzzling her cousin with her sudden glee. "Why didn't she take some of that family recipe Great be talking about? The way Great tell it, that thing can cure cancer."

Cookie laughed then, and it was Gayle's turn to be puzzled. "You can't go by Great. She exaggerates everything—especially the powers of that old recipe."

Why Cookie gotta laugh like that? And to think: Today was gonna be recipe day.

Cookie moved closer to Gayle. "You know how some women just take to mothering?" Cookie rattled on. "They can care for a houseload of children? Not Mama. Mama likes thinking too much to have kids running around every which way."

"So what she be thinking about?" Gayle asked sarcastically.

"Mama teaches history at Columbus College," Cookie said, not catching on to Gayle's sarcasm. "She's writing a book on oral history for her doctoral dissertation. The only thing missing is what Great's got to give."

Even if Gayle had known half of them words Cookie had sputtered out, she refused to be impressed. "I don't see why Auntie got to do all that when she got a big old house, a husband, nice clothes, and a car. I bet she got some kind of mink coat hanging in the closet. That be the uniform for preachers' wives. If I had all that I wouldn't work a lick except to keep my house clean. If Auntie was smart she'd try to have a baby boy so yawl can call him Luther—seeing yawl big on naming everything Luther."

"But Mama can't have no more babies," Cookie insisted in heavy whispers.

Gayle sucked her teeth. "You just glad you the only child, spoiled rotten. Bet Uncle Luther calls you Puddinhead or Princess or some spoiled pet name 'sides Cookie."

"You don't have to be so nasty, Cousin. What did I do to you?"

"With all those peaches hanging in them trees it's a wonder you ain't called Peaches."

Cookie shot Gayle a hard look then tossed her head.

Gayle tossed her head mockingly. "Is that how yawl do it? You'd never survive where I'm from."

Cookie brought the basket into the pantry. Gayle watched the screen door to see if she would come back. Didn't Cookie understand? She was in a talking bitch mood. Dog. The homegirls would understand that. They'd snap and cut up on one another till someone's feelings got hurt good and someone else felt better.

Cookie came back with the last load. Gayle decided she'd let her off easy.

"What do you do for fun besides going to church? Where your friends? Phone ain't rang once for you since I been here. Don't some nigger come honking his car for you?"

"Cousin, your mouth! Why you throw that word around like that?"

Gayle couldn't figure out which word she meant. But this always happened with Cookie. They'd start out having a conversation, but they'd lose each other.

Cookie said her friends and her fun were mainly in church. She said she didn't have a boyfriend, although she dated occasionally.

"Sure you do." Gayle laughed, picturing a church son driving his daddy's wood-paneled station wagon with HONK IF YOU LOVE JESUS on the bumper.

"Or sometimes I pick up my girlfriends and we go to the movies."

"Your Mama let you drive her car?" Gayle asked. Up until now her queries were spiked with meanness. Now she was interested.

"No, that little car over there is mine," Cookie said with pride. "Mama drives the sedan."

"Well, check you out," Gayle said. "I wouldn't mind going for a ride."

"No one is to drive it but me," Cookie said right away.

"Did I say anything like that?" Gayle snapped.

Next thing Gayle knew, Cookie was falling all over her big ox self with apologies. This was going to be too easy, Gayle thought.

"I only mentioned it 'cause I'm running low on diapers," Gayle said. "And I can't be washing those cloth diapers Auntie gave me. Not the way José lets loose."

"Oh, Cousin, I'd be glad to take you to town."

Gayle already seemed to know that.

9

Dear Troy,

By now you shud no Mama gone mad and sin
me an the baby down sowf. I dont got no
monnie an no way back. Sin me some monnie
so I can hop a bus home. Give it to Terri to give
to me. Ther is nothing here to rit about. They
work me hard.

I member the last time we did it. It so good.
Too bad your Mama come home an I had to leve
out the window. That was funny. I am not missing
around with no one.

2 Fly
2 Be
4 Got

Gayle

P.S. Mama took me for the aborshun. No swet.
We can make another baby win I get home.

GAYLE folded and taped the letter, then wrote on the
outside GIVE TO TROY, pressing down so hard the pen
ate through the paper. She had five minutes to write
another letter, then run downstairs before Cookie could
weasel out of giving her a ride into town.

Girlfriend,

We got to talk. For real. Yal must break me
out of here. No TV no music no hanging no
boys. Serious prisin. Can you and Lynda git
up some monnie to sin me? I got to git out of
here.

Keep an eye on Troy make sure he dont talk
to no one wile I'm gone. Tell Vanita you will
hurt her face if she look at him. For real.

Do Big Jose ask about me and his son? Tell
him I met a fine dud with monnie and we
married. Let him suffer.

Tell Joycee hi. If you see Mama dont tell
her sqwat doo doo. You can tell Junie hi if
he aint dead yet. Sike! I'll be back in time
for dubble dutch jump off. See if they still
got my lay-away at the mall. Put a dolar on
it for me.

Peace

Gayle

P.S. The baby gots a toof!

Gayle trotted downstairs and out the door with her letters, her bag, her baby in the baby carrier, and the last of
her money. Enduring José's weight seemed a small price
to pay for some freedom. Finally! She and José were
getting out of the big house, away from the crosses
and headstones, out from under Uncle Luther and Miss
Auntie.

"Can't wait till you walking," she told her son.

He reached for her earrings.

Gayle opened the door to Cookie's car and sat up front
with the baby strapped to her. She rocked back and forth,

saying, "Go, go, go," until Cookie emerged from the house just as slow as she tra-la-la pleased.

Cookie shook her head. "Cousin Gayle, you have to sit in the back."

"Why?"

"No car seat for the baby."

"He's strapped to me in this carrier. I gots on a seat belt. Double protection. See?" Gayle said. "Let's roll."

"I don't think that's a good idea," Cookie said.

"Ain't nothing gon' happen," Gayle snapped. "Now let's go before they holler for me to come in and polish the silverware, the floors, and all fifty doorknobs."

Cookie smiled and with some reluctance started the car. As they drove off, Gayle noted the route into town. The road went on without so much as a bus stop, let alone a gypsy van or subway station. This was hardly South Jamaica, Queens, where all you needed to get around was change in your pocket.

"Don't this car got a radio?" Gayle asked, randomly mashing buttons below the dashboard. Cookie didn't answer, so Gayle kept pushing buttons with one hand until out jumped an AM prophet proclaiming HIS HOLY NAME in her ear. Gayle wrapped herself around the baby, smothering his face with her own. Cookie couldn't help laughing.

"That ain't funny," Gayle cried, uncurling herself from her baby.

Cookie stopped horse-laughing long enough to soften the volume on the radio. "Forgive me, Cousin, but you know it was. Praise God for seat belts. You was headed through the roof."

"Haw, haw." Gayle reached over and clicked on the FM button, then rolled the tuner searching for a familiar beat. To her relief she found it and began singing the lead vocals, the background, and the instrumentals.

"Cousin Gayle, what do you call that noise?"

"Sang—ing" she replied in time with the music.

"You got Gates blood. How come you can't sing?"

"Oh?" came Gayle's attitude. "You sing better?"

"Cousin, you're not bad. You just don't sound any better than this girl on the radio. You know how they all sing. Thin. Nasal. Trying to make up for not having any tone or pitch.'"

" 'Scuse me, Whitney Houston."

Cookie wasn't answering. In fact she looked intense, like she was praying or fighting off an impulse. Gayle took her silence as "shut-up" time and continued to sing.

"How could you not like this group? They fly."

"They're all right," Cookie said. "I just wouldn't want to make my living singing like them."

"You wish you could."

They parked in a minimall. Gayle mailed her letters, then bought a pack of cigarettes, a sweetcake for later, eight jars of baby food, and some diapers. Terri, Lynda, and Troy had to come through with more money. She had already spent the last of what Mama had given her.

"Let's grab some lunch," Cookie said. "My treat."

"Bet."

Cookie directed them to a snack shop. "No, not here," she said as Gayle prepared to sit. "Over here. We can see better." It made no difference to Gayle, who thought Cookie was strange. They sat down at a table and ordered a burger and a tuna melt.

When the waitress set their plates down, Gayle wrinkled her nose at the coleslaw swimming in too much mayonnaise. "Did I ask for that? Looks nasty."

The waitress was caught off guard by Gayle's remark and picked up the dish of coleslaw on Gayle's plate, examining it closely. "Freshly made, baby."

"Ma'am, it's just fine," Cookie assured the waitress. "Just fine." When the waitress went back to the kitchen, Cookie scolded Gayle. "Cousin, you can't go around being ugly just 'cause it suits you."

Gayle shrugged, sliding the coleslaw away from her plate. Even José didn't like its milky looks.

The waitress came back with a high chair for the baby. "Baby, let that big boy sit, so you can enjoy your food."

Gayle began to unharness José, but the waitress did most of it and put the baby in the high chair as well. "That's better," she said and went back to the kitchen.

"Now don't you feel ashamed?" Cookie asked.

Gayle's expression said "not really." She mashed some of her hamburger for José and fed little bits to him. He was more interested in gumming her fingers.

"Hope they got a drugstore in here. I need something for these pains," Gayle said. "You sure Great's recipe fake? Great said it cured her for miscarriages and was good for cramps and all kinds of pains. Wouldn't hurt to cook up a pint."

Cookie stared out the window. Gayle knew she had lost her cousin.

"What's got you so stupid?"

Cookie's eyes were unfocused. She smiled a little.

"Cookie! Cookie!" Gayle turned to see for herself. All she saw was a store—the Sneaker King—and some ox hauling cardboard boxes to the recycling pit. "Cookie, what's with you?"

Cookie's face flushed. "What? I'm sorry, Cousin. You were saying?"

"I was saying I'm hurting and I want to go home. Get with my nigger. Know how long it's been since I had some sex? That's probably why I hurt so bad."

Cookie shushed her cousin. How could she talk like that out loud, in public. Shooting off one word like it was a proper name. Shooting off the other like it was a proper act.

Gayle kept right on talking, feeling free. She was out of the house and unstrapped from her baby.

"Cookie, look me dead in the eye and tell me you don't get hot in the box."

"Gayle, your problem is you're too concerned with"—she wouldn't say it—"that."

"Girlfriend, your problem is you need to think more about *that*," Gayle said. "What's the most you ever done?"

"Nothing."

"Not even a kiss? Come on, Cookie. You nice looking. Sort of. You must be turning someone on."

"Cousin, don't talk so loud!" Cookie said.

"Well?" Gayle whisper-shouted just to be funny.

"You can't tell Daddy."

"Oh, yeah. Me and Uncle Luther tight like sardines."

"I used to date a tenor in the choir. Fred," Cookie said. "Well, one night just out of nowhere, we were talking and he put his mouth on mine and forced his tongue in me. It was disgusting."

"Then what happened?" Gayle pounced.

"Nothing. I pulled away," Cookie said.

"That's it? You serious? He didn't try to suck your titties?"

"No!"

"Or put his fingers down your panties?"

"Gayle, no!"

67

"Okay. When you go to a dance and a boy ask you to slow jam and the music be good and he presses you up on his rod, don't you press hard 'cause it feel good?"

"Cousin Gayle, of course not."

"You know, Cook, you wastin' away. Don't even know what you missing. But find a boy who knows all the moves, all the talk, and forget it. You be dropping your drawers before you know it. That's how José's daddy got me."

The baby started to cry.

"He's teething. Come here, li'l man." She pushed the high chair closer and put her finger in José's mouth. "Once you get that juicy feeling you won't be saying it's disgusting. Old people be saying it's disgusting and wicked 'cause they dried up. But we young, Cookie. We s'posed to have that feeling."

Gayle pushed her plate aside and took out a pack of gum, offering a stick to Cookie, who declined. She stuck one in her mouth and started chewing and popping, a habit from being bored in school.

"Let me tell you what happened. José and his brothers had a bug-spraying business. Don't be thinking my mama keep a bug house, now. So anyway, he'd come by first of the month to do spraying. You should see this guy. He's not all that fine but he got style. He's young. Like twenty. We got to talking 'bout his problems and things just clicked. May sound corny but I'm a sucker for talk and we talked for hours. He'd come first of the month and on nights that Mama worked. He bought me some earrings 'cept they turned. I shoulda known. I'm more mad 'bout those earrings than anything else.

"When I told him about the baby he was all happy, treated me real good. Then he stopped coming. So I sent my girls to find out what's what and they said they saw him at the supermarket with this woman and she fulla belly. So I figure that's his wife. I understood that.

"Last time I saw him was in the hospital. Junie and his friends told him they was gonna hurt him good if he didn't visit me. Junie crazy! Anyway, he showed. Came talking about adoption. Yeah, right. After I tote this sucker in my belly, miss all the dirt going on in school, I'm supposed to give up my baby. Didn't I tell him what to do with his adoption?"

"José's father was your first?"

"I ain't been hoeing around if that's what you mean," Gayle snapped. "'Sides. I didn't go looking for him. He came to me. He was mines."

"But he was married."

"On paper."

"And he gave you those earrings."

"Don't think I forgot."

Cookie stared over at the Sneaker King, where the guy was tearing those cardboard boxes with his hands. After some silence, Cookie asked, "Did it ... hurt?"

"What? Getting busted? Yeah, it hurt. It did! I won't lie. He didn't waste no time getting me ready. He just stuck me like that. It hurted. But that goes away. I didn't bleed much, and it felt good after the second and third go-round. Cookie, how old you? Sixteen? Might as well get it over with—get busted."

"Busted? Cousin, do you hear yourself?" Cookie scolded. "All I know is I'm not doing anything until I'm married. And it won't be about getting busted."

"The more you wait, the more you'll dry up. It'll really hurt then. I'm telling you, Cuz. Do it now while you're young and juicy."

Pop! Gayle's spit on Cookie's arm felt like hot fire. Cookie wiped it away.

At that moment José let out a wail, having been

69

strapped into the high chair long enough. He banged his fat little hands on the tray and pitched from side to side, kicking his legs.

Gayle stamped her feet, unbuckled the high chair straps, and yanked José out, plopping him onto her lap.

"Damn. Can't have a minute of freedom."

Cookie gazed out of the window, over to the Sneaker King. The guy was gone, along with her appetite.

❧ 10 ❧

Gayle didn't see what the fuss was about. It took all of ten minutes to take three peaches, cut them up, and throw the pits in a mason jar along with the fruit and some water. Tear off a strip of Mahalia's bark, add a bit of black licorice, then cover it with one of Uncle Luther's handkerchiefs.

"There. Recipe. Even if it don't heal the woman pains, one sip'll make Great happy. Live that long, you deserve to be happy."

She secured José to her hip and wrapped the mason jar in a towel, which she placed in Great's washbasin. She had to be careful. Uncle Luther had been at Great's bedside since morning.

She entered the room. Her uncle's trunk leaned toward Great, tree to sun, waiting for death to happen. Great lay stiffly, eyes at rest, as if to oblige her grandson.

Startled, he glanced up. His face, dark and square, lengthened with his displeasure in her presence. When he rose to full tower Gayle felt the risk she invited upon herself, sneaking the recipe into Great's room. She pictured Uncle Luther smashing and damning the mason jar, then making her clean the whole mess.

71

"Hey! Whattup?" Gayle trumpeted loud and fresh in spite of herself. She held onto José tightly and beamed straight at Uncle Luther to keep from looking down at the lumpy towel.

"Child, this is a home, not some street. Leave that street talk where you found it."

"Dog. What I do? All I said was hey."

He advanced toward her, his footsteps monster heavy. "And I said watch your mouth."

Gayle came close to sucking her teeth but resisted. No telling what teeth sucking would draw from Uncle Luther.

"Awright." Her version of "Yes sir."

"Your great-grandmother will want to be read to from the Book of Ruth when she awakens. You can read, can't you?"

Kiss my ass, Uncle. You want me to step wrong. You looking to knock my teeth out. But you ain't slick, and I ain't stupid.

"Yeah, I can read."

Gayle hoped Great would come to life and say something snappy to make Uncle look like an overstuffed turkey. Her great-grandmother lay peacefully unaware of everything.

Uncle Luther left the room marching. *He want you to know he come and gone.* When the thunder passed, Great's eyelids rolled up.

"He gone?"

"Yeah."

Gayle sat the baby on the rug and put the basin on the nightstand. "So you just faking? Oughta be 'shamed of yourself."

Gayle believed Miss Great would have laughed but laughing strained her stomach. She did smile though.

"I made up that recipe," Gayle said. "Here it is."

"Won't be long 'fore it's ready," Great said, giving a weak inspection, which consisted mainly of feeling the mason jar. "Set it down in the bureau there. Ain't no'n get to it."

"That thing won't kill you, will it?" Gayle asked.

"Naw," Great said. "It won't have much kick. By the time it ferment I'll be gone to glory. I want a taste is all." She wrapped her fingers around the jar. Gayle noted that the long fingers were much like her own.

José crawled to her sneaker. Gayle bent down and lifted him up onto her lap.

"I can't believe Mama used to make this."

"Ruth Bell and that Ginny girl. Those two rascals. If Little Luther ever knowed they made it for me he'd have a natural fit."

Gayle felt Miss Great was in the talking mood. She propped her up with the pillows.

"D'ain all they made. Ruthie made the love potion to put in Luther's food for Ginny—them being close, like sisters."

"Whut?"

"Now, Luther was much older than Ginny and didn't see her as nothing more than his baby sister's playmate. He was expected to marry a preacher's daughter from Baker and unite the two churches. But Ginny loved herself some Luther and meant to have him for her own."

"What happened? Miss Auntie slugged it out with that Baker gal?"

Great shook her head. "Ruthie'd have Ginny over to supper and sit her in front of Luther while he ate. Luther start to get a little hot under the collar. Never knew what hit him."

"Granny, you pulling my chain. No such thing as love potion."

"I've made potions, healings, salves . . ." Great chanted.

73

"Anything God plant got power to heal. I'm tellin you. Better get what I know. . . . What Mammy Gates knowed. And her before her and so on to the root. We got the healing. We got the healing," she said, trancelike.

Gayle repeated it to herself. "We got the healing. We got the healing."

Great's eyelids flickered. Gayle had to keep her talking.

"Why don't Miss Auntie make that potion? Uncle Luther could use some."

"Was Ruthie had the right sense of things," Great said with a spurt of energy. " 'Sides, with Ginny you had to write things out for. Measure precisely. Ruthie, I could say 'a bit' or 'some' and she'd feel it out. Ginny was just there keeping the secret."

"Do I got the right sense?" Gayle asked, looking at her long fingers. "How'll I know when the recipe's ready?"

"It'll ferment. Change colors. I'll take some on the first change. Won't last for the second."

"How'll I know the first change?"

"Got eyes, ain't you?"

It didn't take long to tire out Great. Sometimes Great was lively, telling her stories. Then she'd seem peacefully weary, ready to slip away. Gayle wouldn't be surprised if Uncle Luther sat at her bed ordering her to die so he could add her bones to the bone patch out front. Good old Great. She probably was hanging on just to have her peach liquor and spite Uncle Luther.

"Miss Great, you all right," Gayle said.

She opened the bottom drawer to the wooden bureau. A strong cedar smell escaped. The drawer hadn't been opened in years. She put the recipe jar in the drawer and closed it quietly. Then she collected her son and went downstairs to the kitchen. Cookie had made a sandwich and said she was going upstairs to sit with Great.

"I don't get it. Every time I go up there, you, Uncle, or Miss Auntie be sitting at Great's bed watching. Not lifting a finger to clean or feed her but yawl be scoping."

Cookie took a healthy bite of her sandwich, chewed, then answered. "Great gotta Tell before she dies."

"Tell what?" Gayle asked.

"The family history," Cookie said.

"Maybe she wrote it down somewhere."

"Oh no," Cookie said. "She'd never do that. Someone's been doing the Telling since we got here, adding more as it goes along. It's like talking to our ancestors."

"I'm sorry, but that sounds creepy. Talking to those dead folks planted in the yard like rutabagas."

Cookie laughed at Gayle. "Cousin, it's who we are."

"Unh-unh. We alive. They dead," Gayle stated flatly. "If you ask me it's stupid. What if Great got hit by a car before she could Tell. Then what?"

"It's supposed to be done by talking," Cookie insisted.

"How you know Great's not senile? Out of all yawl I like her best, but she can't tell me from my mama—and me and Mama don't even favor. How she s'posed to tell you something 'bout hundreds of years ago?"

"Great has it. She told me. When the time is right she'll do the Telling."

"And that's why yawl be guarding her bed—so she could say your great-great-grandpappy be planted next to your great-great-grandmammy?"

"Cousin, our past is in the Telling. Yours too."

"Zat all? I'll save yawl the trouble. Once we was slaves then we got free, ran the white folks out the big house, and took over—teach them who not to mess with. End of story."

Cookie laughed at Gayle's rendition.

"Surprise you to know we shared this house with the

white folks? Um-hm. When the Union soldiers killed off the master, Great-great-great-grandma Mahalia hid and raised the master's son. He grew up and took Mahalia's baby girl for his wife and we've been in this house ever since."

"You lie."

"It's in the family history," Cookie said.

"So you saying we got white blood?"

"Now, Cousin Gayle, look in the mirror," Cookie said.

Gayle sucked her teeth. She could have done without that bit of family history.

Cookie added, "We're direct from Africa too, now. If you read Mama's papers you'd know about the two sisters from Senegal. But like everyone else we got some Indian, some white, but mostly us. You should read the family history, Cousin. That way you can share it with José when he is older. We all know the history. But the one who Tells is the one who holds hands with the past. The past keeps us alive." Cookie was doing a recitation for the school play. Miss Auntie was her drama coach.

Gayle was not interested in the past. Specially not no slavery—though those potions and healing plants sounded interesting. But she had no desire to link hands with the ancestors. They were in the ground where they belonged.

"I'm the one," Cookie said short of a boast.

"One what?"

"The one she going to Tell."

"How do you know?" Gayle said, almost laughing at Cookie's pride and sincerity. Cookie cared so much about the slave days, but she didn't care about what she looked like in kneesocks.

"Great said Mama gonna throw in a book for the whole world to forget. Papa gonna change it to suit the gospel according to Luther. That leaves me to Tell."

76

"And what you gonna do with it? Carry it to your deathbed 'fore spitting it out? So stupid. Over a couple of cabbages planted in the front yard and an old slave house."

Cookie laughed off her cousin's ignorance and took her sandwich up to Great's room.

"Cookie's out of luck if she thinks Great's Telling. Great ain't Telling no one nothing. Know how I know?"

José patted her mouth.

" 'Cause Great stubborn like you and me."

⚘11⚘

"A WHOLE THREE HOURS in church. Can you believe that?"

José kicked his legs, anticipating falling baby powder from above. He clapped, signaling "Me! Me!" as his mother dashed powder down her orange minidress.

"If God everywhere, why can't we pray at home when we feel like it?" She stuffed one last diaper in her shoulder bag, then snapped it shut. "Just answer me that, little man."

Her aunt entered the room carrying a long gray-blue dress and a white slip. "Morning, sweetie," she said, laying the dress out on the bed.

Gayle glanced at her aunt, then at the dress and slip. *Auntie, ya buggin'. For real.*

Miss Auntie cleared her throat. "I said good morning."

"G'mornin," she said to her aunt, who was outfitted in an ivory suit, red pumps, and a summer brim—with a feather, no less. She then glared at the dirt-kissing dress spread out on her bed, its doofy Peter Pan collar and lifeless gray shade. "What's that?"

"Your church dress," Miss Auntie replied coolly.

"Already got one on," Gayle told her aunt.

Miss Auntie stared down her blunt nose at Gayle's bright orange dress. "No, sweetie. That is not a church dress."

"It's the style," Gayle whined.

"I know what it is," Miss Auntie said. "And I know where it's not going." She gave Gayle five minutes to change into the gray-blue dress.

Gayle stepped into the slip, hoping to tear it. She "accidentally" dropped the linen dress, then kicked it up off the floor. She caught it and balled it up, wanting Miss Auntie to start a fight so that she would be left at home.

"You don't want to look like you just rolled out of bed, do you, sweetie?"

Before Gayle could answer, Great's Sunday nurse, Miss Foster, appeared in the threshold, glasses on the tip of her nose. "Mercy, baby! Go'n down the hall and show your great-grandma the old dress still got it."

Gayle sucked her teeth. "I knew it. Dress a hundred years old."

Gayle watched her relatives spring to life as they pulled into the pastor's very own parking space. Especially Miss Auntie, who seemed to grow another three inches on top of her skyscraping self. Miss Auntie lovingly wrapped her arm around her niece and grandnephew, as if she wasn't responsible for having Gayle look like Mammy Yokum, and proceeded with the tour.

"Here is the first brick your grandpa and Great-grandpa Luther laid into the foundation of Freedom Gate Church. Here is the stump from the field where Great-great-grandpa Luther preached during slavery. They had it transplanted, you know. Here is the opened gate, our family symbol . . ."

Don't she know this baby heavy?

Hip shifting, eyeball rolling, and heavy sighing did not deter Miss Auntie from conducting her tour. Gayle was relieved that services were about to begin, so she could sit down.

Uncle Luther was installed on his throne, looking out at his kingdom. The house was packed with high-spirited churchgoers who lived, *lived* for this day.

Cookie sat in the choir pew, another pecan-pie face in a blue satin robe. She smiled in Gayle's direction.

Think she cute. Only reason she up there, her daddy's the pastor.

Two hours fifty-eight minutes to go. During the first prayer she asked that the music be thumping and the choir be jumping. That Uncle Luther wouldn't preach too long and that Miss Auntie wouldn't try to push her up on stage when the call for sinners sounded.

Same people fall out calling "Save me, Jesus" be acting up all over again Monday to Saturday, thinking they foolin' God like He don't have two eyes. That's why you'll never see me jumping up screaming, "Save me, Jesus." I likes cussing and fussing and kicking up dirt, and God knows it.

"Say what, sweetie?"

"Huh? I ain't said nothing."

The service moved slowly. Gayle bounced José on her knees to soothe him until Miss Auntie made her stop. How was she going to get through church without a cigarette or gum?

After nearly an hour of preliminaries, Uncle Luther rose from his throne and ascended the pulpit. Heads leaned forward to receive The Word. When he spoke his voice boomed, filling every corner of Freedom Gate. This is what God must sound like, Gayle thought. Like he could send a flood bursting through the pews.

Cookie was right. Uncle Luther could preach! Wasn't even halfway into the sermon and people were falling out with the hallelujahs. When he pointed from the pulpit, his finger dug into your chest. When he hurled his question down into the congregation, he meant to be answered. And if the response from the congregation didn't resound loudly enough, sincerely enough, he'd go back to the cannon and fire off that question until someone was on his feet—hallelujah—with the right testimony.

Gayle would just as soon keep her testimony to herself. The only exclamation that she felt forthcoming did not belong in church.

José caught the spirit. He threw his hands in the air, smacked his mother in the face, and hollered with all his power. Before Gayle could reach into her shoulder bag for a bottle or a pacifier, a woman usher reached over her and scooped José from her arms. Gayle lunged forward to grab her baby, but Auntie pinned her down.

"He's going to the nursery. Sister Walker will keep him."

"They can't just snatch my baby."

"He'll be fine," Aunt Virginia said quietly. "He can play, get fed and changed. Now hush."

Gayle turned, trying to follow the woman who had marched off with her son. All she caught was the woman's tail so high off the ground it seemed to smack her in the back as she clomped down the aisle in her white marshmallow wedges. José wasn't complaining. In fact, he was trying to gum the baby snatcher's neck when he ought to be wailing for his mama like his sun and stars had been torn from the sky.

Who she think she is snatching my baby?

It was one thing to pass José off on the homegirls

when she got tired of him, but having José ripped from her arms made her face burn.

"Gayle Ann, turn around," her aunt whispered.

Gayle wanted to sink down in the hot pit where her anger pulled her, but Miss Auntie was right there stroking her hand. Then the choir rose in unison. They marched out from the choir chamber in perfectly timed step-bops until all were in place. They formed a wave of blue satin, swaying, moaning softly over the accompaniment of the organ. Cookie now stood apart from the magnificent blue, and took the microphone. With eyes closed and head tilted back, she proceeded to wash over the hot pit where Gayle sank. Gayle resisted Cookie with all her jealous anger, but could not fight the feeling of being lifted by song.

Was that Cookie? Causing all of that?

"Miss Auntie," she whispered, "why Cookie ain't said she could sing?"

"Sweetie, the Lord didn't bless Cookie's voice so she could brag. No. That would be falling to pride, and you know who fell to pride."

"Uh-huh," Gayle lied.

When the service ended, Gayle raised her hand—hallelujah!—truly glad it was over. She shot straight up thinking about the door, the mob, bumming a smoke, then getting her baby. Before she could make a move Miss Auntie grabbed hold of her. "Let me take you around, sweetie. Your mother's friends would love to meet you."

Gayle wasn't in any hurry to meet them. Especially the way they stole glances of her face for their "that's the one" gossip. As if Gayle cared.

"Ginny! Ginny!" called one such starer. "And who might this young lady be?"

"Paulette, dear. How are you? Surely you remember Ruth Bell. This is her daughter, Gayle Ann, visiting from New York."

"Your mother and I went to high school together. Sang in the choir."

Gayle recognized her from the choir, the way her voice pushed itself forward trying to rise above the sopranos. Gave her a headache.

Gayle said, "Yeah, that's nice," but it came off like "Beat it, old bag." Auntie felt it and yanked her arm.

"I expect to see you in the choir, young lady," the woman said.

"I don't sang," Gayle said.

"How can that be?" Paulette gasped, which seemed put on to Gayle. "You're Ruth Bell's baby girl. Singing genes like that don't just die out."

Gayle could really care less. All these people saying how Mama could sing when Mama hated music. Mama always went through the house turning radios off, worried to death about her electric bill.

"I wanna get my baby."

"Your baby? How old are you, child? Can't be more than ten, eleven."

"Get glasses, lady. I'm old enough."

She felt Miss Auntie's hand tightening around her wrist. Paulette sped off to the gossipers, leaving Gayle to endure Miss Auntie's wrath and pointing finger.

In the nursery Gayle tried to be mannerly to Miss Auntie's friends. One of them turned to Miss Auntie and whispered, "Country, ain't she?" Miss Auntie poked the lady. Gayle took José and left the nursery. She knew what the giggling was about. All those black folks from Georgia spoke proper Southern like Miss Auntie. They weren't at all impressed that she was from New York. They all thought like Uncle Luther, who had said at the dinner table, "Blacks in Georgia snatched up opportunities when the crumbs were falling. Only opportunities for blacks in New York is in the street, then six feet under."

There he stood, Uncle Luther, every inch the man of God, greeting his congregation. When he caught sight of her standing thirty feet away with child on hip, he turned his back.

She found Cookie with the other choir members.

"Sang yo ass off, dincha?"

"I'm glad you liked it," Cookie said, not looking directly at Gayle.

What? Cookie was supposed to turn a shade of purple, correct her language, or shush her because God was listening. Cookie wasn't even there. Too busy searching over her cousin's head. She nodded absently and smiled as a cluster of people praised her voice.

Gayle looked around to see who or what had put that dazed expression on Cookie's face.

"What's up with you?"

"Oh, uh, nothing."

Gayle shook her head, took her baby, and searched for Miss Auntie.

12

Gayle swung open the oak doors to Great's wardrobe, not caring if she disturbed Great's sleep. A funk of cedar chips and dried flowers and spices hit her immediately. Her nose wrinkled, her eyelids blinked. She pushed through the musty barrier, shoving the gray-blue dress way, way back where the other dresses could smother it. If that one-hundred-year-old rag didn't feel sunlight until the next century, it would be too soon.

A flicker of pity caught Gayle off guard, as she saw all of Great's finery arranged in the wardrobe, never to be worn by her great-grandmother again. The oak floor was lined with shoes small enough to fit her own feet, and the top shelf was stacked with cardboard hatboxes of varying sizes. On the rack hung coats and dresses, many outfits obviously cut from the same pattern. Fascinated, Gayle ran her fingers along the fabrics. She stroked a marvelous pelt of fur, then brought it out for closer examination, finding a reddish stole with twin fox heads, four paws, and twin tails dangling.

"Gross!" she cried. "You be thinking you high-steppin', wrapped in your fur, and a fox head bites a chunk out your booty." She rehung the stole, exchanging it for a crepe daffodil-colored dress, which she pressed against her body. "Now, why couldn't Miss Auntie find a dress like this?" She put the dress back and turned to Great, who was still sleeping. "You must've been a hot thang," she said, then continued to snoop. Maybe there was money tucked away. A hundred dollars was all she needed for a bus ticket.

She spied a mustard-gold dress bag hanging stiffly at the left end of the rack. Had to be something fabulous, Gayle thought. It was hard to get to. She wrestled it down off the rack and laid it on the floor, kneeling over it while tearing down the zipper. She peeled aside the plastic flap, then snatched her hand away, realizing instantly that the lavender gown with the high neck was Great's funeral gown. Struggling to pull the zipper up, she all but threw it into the wardrobe and turned suddenly. It wouldn't surprise her any to catch the frail woman chuckling.

"That's gonna cost you," Gayle told Great, who slept undisturbed. "Now where you stash your money?"

A wooden cigar box wedged between hatboxes seemed a likely place to start looking. She brought it down and sat over it like a child raking through treasure. There was nothing but letters inside tattered brown envelopes with half-penny stamps dated 1800 something. In one envelope addressed to Mahalia she found what looked like play money. The bills were the wrong sizes, some even dated 1862, with the wrong dead presidents sitting in the wrong corner. She found a five-dollar bill with a buffalo, another bill with women on it. Absolutely useless. She tore the brittle envelopes as she stuffed the phony bills back inside. Next she picked up a handkerchief coarse with cotton seeds woven into its fabric. When she untied it all she found was a tiny cowrie shell, the kind those

"Back to Africa" girls string in their dreadlocks. She rolled it between her finger and thumb, wondering what made the shell so precious. She knotted the handkerchief as she had found it and put it back in the box. Something else caught her eye: a piece of ledger paper torn like it had been stolen from its book. She made out:

1 barrel coffee beans
2 kegs cane likker
1 nigra breed sow 14 yrs old good teeth Bambera stock

Nothing. She put the lid on the cigar box and slid it between the hatboxes, convinced that none of its contents were of value.

She moved on to the dresser, where photos of relatives dead and living tried to shame her for stealing. She stared them down. *What Great gonna do with her money? Go to Atlantic City?*

The top drawer was filled with cotton gowns, and the bottom drawer hid the recipe. She pulled out the drawer second from the bottom, glancing in the mirror to see if she had been caught. Great was still sleeping, so she continued. There was no money hidden in the drawer, only spools of thread, patches of fabric, old dress patterns, and a leather-bound book. She sat down with the book. In its heavyweight black pages were yellowed photographs, newspaper clippings, and funeral cards. The first photograph was of a baby girl hanging onto her mother's long skirt. The next picture was of the same girl, about ten, wearing a raggedy dress with a torn ruffle. *Abigail Coston* was written on the photograph's yellowed border. She was like Gayle: Devil brewing in her eyes, heinie two seconds off a beating. By the time Gayle turned to the wedding photograph, she realized Abigail was Great. She admired her wedding outfit, her long black skirt and white ruffled blouse, her hair gathered and rolled high along the sides. The man who stood with her clutching a Bible to his chest had the same godly preacher face as Uncle Luther but with more Indian features.

Gayle turned the page. Abigail sat with a robust baby boy in her lap while her husband stood. The only smiling face belonged to the boy—grandaddy she never knew. Each turning page told who owed what to which family members. Gayle licked her chipped tooth vainly, pleased she was the only one to inherit Great's petiteness, her features, her ways. Mama got her bigness from Grandaddy and her stone face from Great-grandaddy. Junie would carry his weight like Great-grandaddy if he'd straighten up. Cookie owed every ounce of pretty to her grandmother. But José! José was each and every baby boy Luther, particularly around the mouth and jaw.

She forgot about being up to no good, snooping for money. Great startled her by calling out, "Who that?" Gayle slammed the book shut and shot straight up. "It's me, Miss Great. Just looking for your change of clothes."

"I don't need changing."

"Thought you might."

Great patted the side of the bed, beckoning Gayle to sit with her. "What you need, child?"

Gayle joined her great-grandmother, bringing the book with her. She had been caught and was now relieved. "Miss Great, I need some money."

"Right there in the Bible. Take it."

Gayle grabbed the Bible that sat on Great's nightstand. A ten-dollar bill fell out of Corinthians One. She fanned the pages looking for more. Ten dollars was all there was.

Great inquired about church. Gayle relayed everything, starting with " 'Scuse me, Great, but that gray dress ugly" on to the usher who snatched her baby, her version of

Uncle Luther's sermon, the Paulette snake woman, how Cookie sang the roof off the church, and how weirdly Cookie was behaving lately. "Nose open wide," Great said, which Gayle refused to believe. Cookie in love? No. Great instructed her to "watch and see." Great appreciated the talk, filling in morsels for Gayle to digest. It hurt Gayle to learn that the baby snatcher was her own father's cousin. She and José were joined to yet another branch of family she knew nothing of.

Gayle brought forth the leather-bound book and turned to Great's girlhood pictures.

"Why your dress torn? What you been up to?"

Great strained to look. "Them Hog Pen Hanleys."

"Who?"

"Hog Pen Hanleys, that's who. Smell like they been rolling in their pappy's hog pen. Always pulling my braids, spinning rhymes on my ma and pa. One day I got the biggest Hanley gal by the tuft of her hair and pulled till she had enough. Her brothers ran off and left her. Pa thought it was funny. He owned the general store and photographed me right there grinning with my dress torn. Then he whupped me for fighting in my school dress."

"Great, you's awright." Gayle beamed. She turned to the wedding picture. "How come you married that old man? I thought he was your daddy."

"That old man my Luther," Great said with pride. "I thought Mr. Luther fit to marry Ma but seemed all those meetings were over me. M'tears ain't even dried and I woke up married to Luther, a widower past forty. No children though. Lost them all to the pox. I asked him if Ma could live with us. He said with his mama there, and my mama there I'd never be a wife and it was important I learned wifing and mothering from Miss Mahalia—his mama. I didn't want to know about wifing and mothering, so I ran away three times. Begged Ma let me in. Last time she locked her door. Said I was acting a little girl playing runaway and if I really wanted to run off I would do it right and go to Texas or some far-off place like that. 'Take care,' Ma said. 'Those out-west Indians not as kindly as the ones down here. They might see your black hide and hunt you like a buffalo.'

"Ain't never been out the county. Frightened me so bad I ran home to Luther. Was simple enough to tell him what Ma said and he laughed at me. I got to noticing how handsome his face was when he laughing, and I never ran from him again. Ripened three times, but only one child lived to be a man. Another Luther. My Sonny. Your granddaddy.

"Now, Sonny spread the Word, like all them Luthers before him. Sonny a marching preacher. All those Civil Rights marches ... Selma, Wash'ton, Miss'sippi! Sonny was right there, marching and preaching. Among men he stood out like a giant! Praise God! You'da loved your grandpa. He could laugh big, talk big. Get the people moving. But Sonny got stopped by the law driving up from Alabama from one of them marches. Seems they didn't like the looks of a big cullud man in a Thunderbird. And Sonny couldn't play boy to save his life. He was just too tall for alla that ..." Sorrow took Great away momentarily. Gayle touched her cheek softly and she came back. "Your Uncle Luther was about your age when we put him on a train to Alabama to get the car and drive his daddy's body home. My Luther couldn't make the trip. His time was coming. He was too old. Kept saying over and over that with Sonny gone, he had to Tell me."

"The Telling?"

"The Telling," Great rejoined. "Wasn't s'pose to go to

me. S'pose to pass down to all them Luthers. The ones could preach the Word. Child! That Ginny girl liked to worry me to death 'bout the Telling. Something about 'orah histry.' I got so scared of her prodding me with recorders and cameras that I wouldn't say a word."

Gayle shook her head, smiling. "Stubborn."

"He told me, over and over, like the Spirit moving his lips. Then he passed. Never did see Sonny. Not in this life."

"They went together?"

"Oh, yeah," Great said, filled with genuine joy. "Big old send-off. Preachers came far as Ohio. Old Luther and Sonny brought out the finest preaching. And the eulogies! Freedom singers came from Canaday to sing jubilations. And the stove burned night and day, feeding all the people that filled the house. That was a good time!"

"Great, if anything happened to José I'd have to kill somebody."

"Baby, why you want to say a thing like that?"

"Miss Great, you happy they died?"

"Oh, no, baby. That grieved me the most. But I knew they was in paradise and that ain't a cause of grief."

Gayle shook her head. "Yawl put too much in this glory, glory business. You won't see me jumping up and down when it's dying time. Not like you. Great, you just as happy it's around the corner."

"Amen, glory, glory," Great said. "And I wants a happy send-off with singing I can hear from beyond. People coming by the house filling it with life. Just throw a nice little dress on me. Nothing fussy and high tone, but no sackcloth either. Then on to paradise."

"How you know you going to paradise, Miss Great?"

"Baby, I'm as good as gold. But shinier."

Gayle laughed.

"Oh, I was a young devil," Great admitted. "But I got the goodest heart. Ain't never turned away a soul in need, and I gave the world my only son—that's how I know! Gold," she said patting her breast lightly. "Good as gold."

"Good like Cookie."

Great thought for a while then answered, "Cookie a good child. Yes, she is. Good is all she knows. Now, you'sa devil. But that's all right. When you lay down your deviling, you won't turn back and can't no one turn you. You'll be stronger than those who lived by the rule all their lives. Paradise will open for you, too."

Gayle sucked her teeth. "Ain't going to paradise no time soon, Granny."

"Don't worry none," Great said. "Paradise ain't having you no time soon. Now, let's check on the recipe 'fore they come."

❧13❧

José threw his pacifier down on the kitchen floor for the third time, squealing and banging his hands on his high-chair tray.

Gayle slammed her hand on the kitchen table and pulled back her chair, leaving a skid mark. "Stop it, José! I'm not playing with you," she warned.

He responded with a *pat-a-tat-tat-tat* on his tray, looking up at her with love in his eyes.

"Lookit what you made me do," she said of the floor mark, knowing she'd have to scrub and wax it later. "You think that's funny, don't you."

Miss Auntie, who up until now had been sitting quietly at the breakfast counter, cleared her throat. As far as Gayle was concerned, Miss Auntie could take her criticizing grunts and those papers she was marking over to another corner of the house. It wasn't like Miss Auntie had sweated out seven hours of hard labor bringing José into the world.

Gayle retrieved and rinsed the pacifier one last time. She aimed her finger at her son and told him, "I'll fix you good." It was all she could do to keep from unloading her mind, feeling Miss Auntie's eyes crawling up her

93

back. She kept cool, taking out a diaper pin from the curio jar that sat on the sink counter, and fastened the pacifier to José's bib. Frustration overwhelmed him. He tugged on the blue plastic loop and looked up at his mother with defiant eyes she could swear were her own.

It gave her profound satisfaction to say, "That's why I'm the mama and *you* the child" when she sat down to finish polishing the silver teapot.

Cookie stepped lively into the kitchen from outside, planting a big kiss on her mother's cheek and heaping unbearable doses of cheer on Gayle and José. She took a glass from the cabinet and the pitcher of lemonade from the refrigerator. For every action—the pouring, the closing of the refrigerator door, the twirling—Cookie had a melody.

José gurgled, hoping Cookie would include him in her play. Gayle rubbed the teapot harder, wanting to be left out.

Don't Cookie know what day it is? All that singin' and slippin' and slidin' like she in a parade! If she had to change sheets, nurse Great, watch the baby, and polish some old 1830-who-gives-a-damn-teapot, Cookie'd know it was Monday. Slave day.

Gayle couldn't stand it any longer. Cookie's joy was overflowing. "All right," Gayle relented. "Whu'sup wit you?"

"It's going to be a great day!" was the best Cookie could do.

Gayle dipped her sponge into the pink cream, sorry she asked in the first place. "I hate Mondays. Reminds me I gotta be here another week with no parole."

Brightness welled and released in Cookie's eyes and spread to her cheeks. She plunked herself before Gayle, rapped her knuckles against the table, and declared,

"Cousin Gayle, you've got to come to fellowship with me."

Miss Auntie confined her comment to a raised eyebrow. Gayle was inclined to agree with her aunt: Cookie must be crazy.

"Churchie meetings? Whatchall do? Talk about bad kids gon' fry in hell?"

Cookie laughed. "Don't be so closed minded, Cousin. I'm talking about a good time. Meeting in town with kids our age. Discussing Scriptures, praying, singing. Just being renewed in Christ!"

In the midst of flagrant eyeball rolling, Gayle caught Miss Auntie smiling. She couldn't figure whether her aunt was amused by Cookie's absolute faith or by the unlikelihood of Gayle's being renewed by anything vaguely spiritual.

Cookie went on, her head lolling from side to side. "We have dances, picnics, guest speakers. And twice a year we go on *retreat*," she emphasized, hoping the retreat would change Gayle's opinion. Having no idea what a retreat was, Gayle remained unreachable, annoyed that her cousin had interrupted her misery with utter stupidity. Gayle concluded the retreat had to do with praying and Scriptures and all those shalt nots.

"I guarantee you'll come away from one meeting high on the Lord," Cookie said, her pie face now fit to burst.

Gayle's neck jerked back. "High on the Lord?" She hadn't begun to contemplate just how simple her cousin was when Cookie added, "It's a nice little drive into town."

Gayle stopped polishing. *Car, drive, the hell out* registered quickly.

"Can we stop at the store on the way back?" Gayle

asked weakly, saving her energy for scheming to get cigarettes and Dairy Queen sundaes out of Cookie.

"You know we can."

Gayle sought out her aunt. "Miss Auntie," she whimpered, altogether too pitifully and too quickly to fool anyone, "can you watch the baby while I go?"

Miss Auntie, her two cents now overdue, laid her pen down on the table. "Now, now, Miss Gayle. I believe I made myself clear. Emanuel is your little bundle of fun. Take him with you."

"All right. All right," Gayle snapped, stamping her feet under the table. For the moment, she was sick of José's drooling looks-like-his-daddy's face. She stuck the sponge down into the pink cream. "He's gotten so big with yawl feeding him everything in creation. He don't walk and I ain't got no stroller. Carrying kids around is backbreaking work."

"Carrying them is easy. Raising them is backbreaking joy," Aunt Virginia rejoined lyrically. "But you're doing just fine, sweetie. Just fine. Now, go see about Great and I'll finish up in here."

It would be easier if Miss Auntie would kick up a storm or had a big old ugly mouth like Mama. Mama could holler! Miss Auntie's voice dipped, making it hard to stop listening to her magic even when she was getting you sick.

This time Gayle sat in the backseat with José rather than giving Cookie a hard time. Cookie a natural fool for Jesus, Gayle thought. Check her out. Praying while the motor warming up. Popping a Jesus tape into the stereo. Singing along and getting happy.

Cookie peered into the rearview mirror and saw Gayle falling into the wave of the gospel chorus crackling through the speakers. "Didn't I tell you this was going to be a great day?"

"It'll do," Gayle said, not wanting her cousin to get the wrong impression. Gayle refused to let the lack of a hip-hop beat dampen her celebration, and accepted that the Clark Sisters, the Mighty Clouds of Joy, and the Winans were as funky as Cookie's stereo got. So what if they weren't out on an all-day stroll up and down Jamaica Avenue or sitting on her stoop waiting for Troy. It was a nice ride into town.

The meeting was held in the church basement, which was packed with young people. Cookie introduced Gayle and José (whom she called Emanuel) to the cluster of kids that grew around them. Most of them were teens; some of them were college students. Every one of them was brimming with spirituality, punctuating every other phrase with "Praise Jesus!" or "Praise God!" Gayle, how-ever, couldn't see herself jumping into that bag, and kept her greetings simple: "Peace, yawl."

No one could Praise the Lord as naturally and as often as Cookie. Look at Miss Cookie, working her show, Gayle thought, both envying and enjoying her cousin's popular-ity. Cookie stayed fixed in the center. A queen bee. The way she reached out and touched hands or waved to jubi-lants across the room, you'd think they'd gathered in her honor. Cookie was actually fascinating, and could say some funny things. All she needed was a new hairstyle, a little makeup, and to burn those clothes—starting with those kneesocks—all things calling for the aid of a girlfriend.

Suddenly, before Gayle's eyes grace turned to clumsi-ness. Cookie bumped into the table where the punch bowl sat, stepped on someone's toes, then ran into the bathroom.

What was her problem? Only thing happened was a guy who was as big as an ox stood in the doorway looking for someone. Gayle recognized him: the Sneaker King dude.

Finally Cookie came out of the bathroom and stood by the punch bowl.

"Who that?" Gayle said, pointing.

"Who?" Cookie asked, staring down at the bowl.

"Stiff Wood, that's who."

"What?"

Again Gayle pointed. "That big dude standing at attention in the back."

"I thought you New Yorkers were supposed to be so cool," Cookie hissed. "And don't point like that," she said, grabbing hold of Gayle's hand. "He'll know we're talking about him."

"Scoop! Scoop! Give up the scoop."

"There's no scoop," Cookie said. "Now keep your voice down. That's not what we're here for."

"How long you been liking Stiff Wood?"

"What makes you think I like him?"

"What makes you think I'm stupid? Dog, Cookie. I may have failed math twice but I can figure. Almost peed on yourself minute he come in the place. Give up the scoop."

"You're not going to lower your voice until I talk, are you?"

"At least you understand me. Talk."

"Okay. Okay." She pulled Gayle aside and spoke in whispers. "His name is Stacey Alexander. He's a freshman at Columbus College where Mama teaches."

"I'm real impressed," Gayle deadpanned.

"He works part time at—"

"The Sneaker King," they said in unison.

"I see him there when I go into town to do my mission work. Oooh! And he's on the football team. I'm sure he'll make varsity next year, probably transfer to Auburn. Cousin, you should see how he looks in his football uniform."

"Why, Miss Cookie, I didn't know you had it in you, but I'm glad you do," Gayle said. Cookie shushed her, but Gayle went right on talking. "So what you gonna do about it, girlfriend?"

"Do?"

"Must be an echo. I said, you like him. He must like you, the way he looking over here every three minutes. Do something. Go on over there and say 'praise the Lord' or whatever yawl say to get that rap going."

Before Cookie could remind Gayle of their reason for attending the meeting, he was standing before them, showing Cookie his big dimples.

"Hello, Sister Constance."

Okay. He fine, Gayle thought, making no secret of checking him out. And he got a deep voice. And he fills out his dungarees and shirt. Yup, she thought, I know zactly what the kiddies'll look like.

Cookie could only smile.

"'Sup, slick? I'm Gayle."

Gayle's brazenness set off panic in Cookie, forcing her to find her tongue before Gayle spoke again. "This is my cousin Gayle from New York."

"Nice to meet you, Gayle," he said. "Baby-sitting?"

Gayle sucked her teeth. "Do I look like I'm baby-sitting? He's mines," she said, thinking, Sho'nuf stiff wood.

He apologized to Gayle but without taking his eyes off Cookie. "Your solo was very moving, Sister."

"Can't she sang?" Gayle chimed in.

Cookie gave Gayle a look. "I sing the same solo the first Sunday of every month."

"You don't have to be modest," he said.

What was Cookie's problem? She couldn't even go eye to eye with him, let alone keep him talking. After Stacey had said his little say he sat with some of the guys while Cookie sat far away.

Later, at the Dairy Queen, Gayle said, "Cookie, you ain't slick."

"What do you mean, Cousin?"

"Even have the nerve to look innocent. 'High on the Lord.' High on Stiff Wood is more like it."

"I go for spiritual renewal."

"And Stiff Wood."

"His name is Stacey Alexander." Cookie tried indignation.

"Was that a sigh I heard?" Gayle teased.

Cookie refused to answer.

"He take your number?"

"No."

"He ask you out?"

"No."

"He's got a woman," Gayle told her cousin. "Don't he, li'l man?" José was asleep, his head on his mother's chest. Gayle wiped the drool from his chin.

"How do you know?"

"He's in college. He's a jock. Got a job. And he's what, eighteen? He's got a woman."

"You're just saying that," Cookie said, though it was clear she wanted to talk more about Stacey Alexander. "Isn't he nice?"

"Nice and built," Gayle said.

"See how you are!" Cookie cried. "I can't tell you anything."

100

"Who you gon' tell if you don't tell me? Your diary? 'Dear Dead Diary,'" she drawled, "'Today Stiff Wood said I sing nice. Then we said hallelujah and we was in heaven.'"

Cookie started laughing.

"Stick with me, and I'll have Stiff Wood eating out of your hand."

❧14❧

GAYLE sat at Great's bedside with José in her lap. "Miss Great, you right."

"Um-hm."

"Cookie in love. Nose wide open. That's why she acting so stupid."

"Um-hm." Miss Great's eyes closed and her breathing became heavy.

"Don't go. Not yet. Miss Great!" Gayle said, rubbing her arm gently. José liked this rubbing game and lunged forward to touch his great-great-grandmother. Gayle caught him in time and held him more securely. She resumed rubbing Great's arm although it did no good. Miss Great had slipped off into one of her journeys and wasn't coming back until she was good and ready.

Gayle remained at her bedside, fingers cupping Miss Great's cheeks. She studied Great's peaceful face, knowing that this would be her death face. The darkness that ringed Great's eyes told all. Great would soon leave her alone in that big house with no one to talk to.

Why did Miss Great have to tire out? They were having a good long talk that morning. Gayle had presented the mason jar, holding it up to the light for Great's approval. Miss Great praised the aroma and color of the concoction. She praised Gayle's good sense for measuring, then praised her hands, describing them as "fine, turning, easing, midwife hands." Normally Gayle would have been full of quips, but that morning she sat quietly and bathed in Great's words. The last—and perhaps only—persons to list her good qualities had been Troy, and before him José.

She held up the mason jar one last time to search for signs of readiness. Great said her senses were sharp. She'd be able to see the first and second changes on her own.

Footsteps marched up the stairs. Gayle froze, fearing Uncle Luther would swing open the door, catch her with "hoodoo juice," and smash the jar on the floor in the name of God before making her clean it up. He was that mean. He would smash Great's last joy just because it was in Gayle's hands and he hated the sight of her and her baby.

She stopped thinking and listened. She heard not marching, but hopping, like somebody was happy. *Happy? Cookie.* She returned the jar to the dresser drawer and pushed it closed.

Cookie stuck her face in the room. She was one big grin.

"Cousin, Great been sleeping long?"

Gayle shook her head. "She'll be out a good while."

Cookie motioned excitedly. "Come see what I brought you."

It had been a long time since someone had brought her anything. Gayle put José on her hip and followed Cookie.

"It's in the car," Cookie said.

"Shoot! Something good, something good."

"Car seat for the baby," Cookie blurted. "Sister Taylor said she won't need it anymore and it's practically new."

Gayle squinted her eyes and wrinkled her nose. "It ain't no stroller."

"I thought you might want to go for a ride," Cookie said, "and I can't drive without a car seat for the baby."

"Awright. Where to?"

"The mall."

Gayle's eyes now sparkled. "Whyn't you say so? My pockets are empty but I'll hang out." She put one arm around Cookie. "Listen, Cookie, I know you got one of those credit cards. Charge me up a Walkman and I'll pay you back."

"Cuz, you can use my Walkman."

"Bet to that!" Gayle fired off. "First stop, the record store for some tapes, 'cause you don't have what I want."

"What. Rap?"

"For starters."

"Don't you get tired of that? Sex, guns. People being rude and crude and proud of it. Do you hear the names they call each other? Would you like to be called a, a . . ."

"Say it, Cookie, say it. Say it, Cookie, say it!" Gayle taunted.

"Not me," Cookie said. "You won't catch that talk coming out of my mouth."

Gayle laughed. "Don't you ever feel like a bitch? I know I do."

"No," Cookie said.

"And I suppose you never get hot for sex?"

"Is that all those songs have to say? I don't know if I should let you borrow my Walkman."

"I know you're joking. Nobody can be that corny," Gayle said. "Now wait while I run up and get my bag."

We rolling! Gayle thought as they left the house behind them. She wriggled in her seat, enjoying the freedom of having her lap to herself, her hands idle, as her eyes grew big with the open road. Life should always be this good. Gayle turned to see how José was getting along in the car seat. That was the first and last time she checked on him as they sailed down the highway.

"Hey! Isn't that the mall back there? We passed it."

"Oh, we're not going to that one," Cookie told her. "Crossing the line to Phenix City, Alabama."

"Alabama!" Gayle said. "How far's that from New York?"

Cookie shook her head, not knowing how far to take Gayle's ignorance. "Relax, Cousin. It's just a few exits off the highway."

"What's wrong with the mall in town?" Gayle asked.

"I can't go to that one. Everyone knows me," Cookie explained.

"Oooh, Cook-eee! Whatchoo up to? Fun at last."

Cookie became unusually serious. "You promise not to tell?"

Gayle fake-slapped the air. Didn't Cookie know the only person worth talking to was dying?

"If you want some condos I'll get them."

"Condos?" Cookie asked.

Cousin was just too slow. "Erection protection," Gayle said. "You know about protection, don't you?"

"Apparently you don't," Cookie shot back.

Gayle loved it when Cookie tried to get snappy. It was like being with the homegirls. Kind of. "Do too. It's not my fault Troy got supersperm."

"No such thing," Cookie said. "I suppose José's father had supersperm too."

"Sho did. There's proof," she said, pointing to her son, who was fast asleep in his car seat.

"I'm not shopping for condoms, Cousin. *Condoms*. I want something else."

"What's in here you can't buy at home?"

Cookie turned with a devilish grin. "Jeans. Stretch jeans."

Gayle stared blankly. "Slow up, Cuz. They got stretch jeans at the mall in Columbus."

"Gayle, I thought you knew. Even though the church says we can now wear pants and makeup, I can't be the first one running to The Gap in lip gloss."

"Why bother?" Gayle asked. "You won't wear them out nowheres. Just a waste of money."

"I know it makes no sense, but it's something I've always wanted. Just for me. I'll be happy to wear them in my room."

"You lying."

"What?"

"You ain't buying no jeans to hang up in your closet. You buying those jeans to shake your booty for Stacey. You ain't slick."

"Unh-unh," Cookie protested, though unable to hide her smile. "This is about me."

They entered The Gap. Cookie strolled around the bins, looking but not touching. Gayle headed straight to the bins of stretch jeans and began riffling through. She picked up a pair of size fourteens and held them up for Cookie.

"Don't you think we should get sixteens?" Cookie asked.

"Fourteen," Gayle insisted. "You're bricked out, but you ain't moose size."

"Don't you think they'll be too tight?"

Gayle ignored Cookie and flagged down a salesgirl. "Yo, girlie."

"What are you doing?" Cookie was mortified. The salesgirl was speeding their way, donning her helpful smile.

"Tell homegirl sixteen is too big."

The salesgirl immediately sided with Gayle. She brought Cookie a selection of cotton jeans to try on. "You'll like these better. Besides, tight's out. These are in. Try them."

Gayle grabbed the jeans with one hand and led Cookie to the fitting room. She let José down on the carpet. He made friends with the baby in the mirror.

"They're too tight," Cookie said.

"Unh-unh. All we gotta do is pull. Once you get 'em on and break 'em in they'll be good. Come on, pull," Gayle said. "Dog, Cookie, you stacked like Jack."

They laughed and pulled until they succeeded in getting them up all the way. Cookie sucked in while Gayle zipped. José clapped hands against the carpeted floor watching his mommy play. Biting her knuckles, Cookie peered sheepishly in the mirror.

"Go'n, girl. Strut."

"No."

"Go 'head," Gayle scolded. "We sure didn't cross two towns for nothing. Go'n. Let's see what you got."

Cookie wouldn't move.

"Go 'head, Cookie. They only pants—and they not even the kind you fry in hell for wearing. These are old granny bloomers if you ask me. Go ahead. Walk. They ain't all that tight."

"You sure?"

"Those things so loose you could squeeze another leg in there."

Cookie dragged her feet across the small fitting room admiring herself in her cotton jeans. No sooner had she struck a somewhat confident pose than Gayle sang out, "She's a brick house—ow!"

"Stop that!" Cookie said, laughing.

They paid for the pants and bought a tape at the record store. Cookie guarded her Gap bag under her arm, feeling thoroughly victorious. Gayle just shook her head and thought, All that for jeans to hang in her closet.

"Next thing we gotta work on is burning those kneesocks," Gayle said.

As they drove out of the parking lot Gayle spun the tuner, searching for music with a hip-hop beat. Cookie told her it was two stations over to the right.

"Cook, you's all right," Gayle said.

"Why, thank you, Cuz."

"Wait till Stiff Wood sees you in those jeans. Girlfriend, you'll be in serious trouble."

"Not me," Cookie sang.

"Hmp. You watch. Stiff Wood will be asking you out."

"Nooo."

"See, look. Here's how we'll play it," Gayle said. "We'll go to the next church meeting. Slick'll come over and say, Sister Constance, you sing like a angel—or some stupid thing like that. Then I'll say, "Yo, slick. Have you seen the new Whoopi Goldberg picture playing in town? I was just telling girlfriend here it'll make you laugh, cry, and pee all at once."

"You wouldn't!" Cookie gasped. "You wouldn't!"

"Don't thank me," Gayle said as she draped her arm over Cookie's backrest. "Just think, Cuz. You and me, me and you. Hanging out. Like sisters on the homefront, looking out for each other."

"And the baby."

"And the baby."

❦15❦

"I DON'T UNDERSTAND YOU, Cuz," Gayle said, brushing Cookie's hair. "After weeks of plotting, we got Stiff Wood right where we want him and you go 'viting him over to meet Auntie and Uncle. You crazy?"

Cookie replied with an air about her, "I won't go out with anyone who won't meet Mommy and Daddy. Besides," she said, admiring her new hairstyle, pulling her bangs more front than side, "I love when Daddy puts terror in their hearts."

"But they won't make a move."

"Exactly," Cookie said, beaming.

Gayle swept Cookie's bangs off of her face. "Cuz, look in my eyes and tell me you don't want that boy to touch you."

Cookie raised her chin. "That's not on my mind."

Gayle slapped Cookie's shoulder, then resumed brushing. Hard. "It's on mine. I misses Troy. I could use some good sex, way yawl got me slaving. Shoot. I need to feel good," she said. "Troy's up there screwing around. I know he is. If I don't get back to New York . . ."

Gayle's free and unrepentant talk of sex stifled the sisterhood trying to grow between them. Cookie sat tense, unable to offer that little sound, that um-hm girlfriends feed each other.

Cookie changed the subject. "You know, Cuz," she said, "I plan to see New York someday."

"Now you're talking," Gayle exclaimed. "We could drive up in your car and stay with my friends. We could have a hot time. You and me, Cook."

"And the baby."

"Goes without saying," Gayle replied, hating her cousin's constant need to correct her.

While Gayle made plans to escape, Cookie fantasized about Radio City, the Apollo, and the Metropolitan Opera. "It's a shame you never knew Grandmama. She had a true gift for opera. Her dream was to sing *Aïda* at the Metropolitan. Once she took me to the Springer Opera House when Jessye Norman was in town and ..."

Gayle left Cookie at the opera. Her thoughts had gone to the soft spot on Troy Mama couch, then to lying with Troy in the marshy grass at Baisley Park where those pond mosquitoes ate her butt. She sighed. The good old days ...

Cookie hadn't stopped talking. Something 'bout some Schomburg whatever. Gayle refused to let it fog up her picture of the real New York, which had nothing to do with the Metropolitan Opera, the Apollo, Radio City, and all. No. The real New York jumped to fireworks going off on the block, in the projects, on the Avenue.

See, Cookie. I hate you. I throw you some solid girl talk and you go saying something stupid like "high on the Lord" or "opera."

Gayle's sneer stopped Cookie's chatter. She changed her tune. "All that New York talk is well and good, but I'm not leaving Great till she ready to leave me."

Gayle eyed her squarely. "Step off the bull. You ain't

110

sat at Great's bed since Stiff Wood jumped into the picture. You don't even care if she Tells or not."

"And you do?"

"All I know is you only have eyes for Stiff Wood."

"That's not—"

"Go 'head, Cook. Let me catch you lying."

Cookie finally admitted to liking Stacey, prompting Gayle to add, "Liar. You don't like him. You *love* Stiff Wood. Honestly, Cook. You so stupid lately I know it's about Stiff Wood."

"His name is Stacey. Why do you have to be so ugly?"

Gayle looked in the mirror. *Who she calling ugly?*

Cookie looked at Gayle. Why couldn't she understand? "It's not easy living with this great big voice. It's as if it doesn't even belong to me. Everyone expects so much. But Stacey ... Stacey looks at me for me."

Cookie was laughable. Stacey hadn't cracked his wallet open for homegirl, bought her any gold favors, or laid her down, and Cookie was rambling like he the king.

"Did you tell him you gon' be an opera singer?"

"Go ahead. Laugh, why don't you?" Cookie said. "What do you know about a decent friendship with a boy anyway? It's the little things about Stacey. ... The way his hands make mine look tiny—"

"Oh, shoot! Stiff Wood kissed you, didn't he? That's why you acting silly talking about opera. So how was it? Does he got that juicy tongue or is it dry like sandpaper?"

Cookie yanked her head away from Gayle. "Cuz, you're disgusting."

"Be that way," Gayle said. "Brush your own greasy head."

What was wrong with Cookie? Why couldn't she do her part like a real girlfriend and share Stacey? After all, Gayle shared Troy and José with the girls. Repeated all their talk, her fresh responses, played back all their moves, her appraisals.

"All I asked is if he could kiss. Dog."

"If you must know, he kissed me on my cheek and on both hands," Cookie said, maintaining her air.

"Get outta here! What's wrong with him? Honestly, Cook. Little kids do that kind of no-kissing."

"So."

"So? When Stiff Wood gets here, what yawl gon' do? Look at your baby pictures and play checkers on the porch? I saw that on a movie 'bout some old folks home."

"Haw, haw. Very funny," Cookie said. "But you won't find my belly sticking out because some guy kissed me. I'm no fool."

Gayle almost choked laughing. They were friends again. "Cuz! You snapped back!"

"That's right," Cookie said. "So don't mess with me."

Gayle laughed and laughed, banging Cookie on the head with the brush between each "ho!" As big as Cookie was, she believed in turning the other cheek and being nicey-nice. Schooling Cookie would take time.

When Stacey arrived, Gayle withdrew from the cast of characters who performed on his behalf. They were putting on extra just because Stacey Alexander was taking Cookie to the movies. Cookie was extra joyous, humming and bumping into things. Miss Auntie was extra grand and sweet, full of sayings meant to make you toss your head back and laugh. Uncle Luther paced louder than usual, his face tighter than ever. Even José was full of cooing and slobbering because Stacey lifted him up and flew him around airplane style.

It was all disgusting. Cookie kept prancing around Uncle Luther with little thises and thats about Stacey hoping to sway him, but Luther wasn't about to just hand over his daughter. Uncle Luther took aim at all those Stacey thises and Stacey thats like he was shooting crows off a clothesline. He thought it was good that Stacey was in college, but he had no regard for athletes. "God endows a man with physical abilities and man abuses it with drugs, immorality, and pride. Is this how you repay your Father?" Stacey returned respectfully but firmly that he got into school with what God gave him—his family not having been blessed with either money or position. Miss Auntie and Cookie praised God and Stacey and grinned and kicked feet under the table like they had snuck an expensive dress home from the mall and ripped off the price tag.

Instead of telling her folks to back off, Cookie beamed while her parents stole the show. Miss Auntie kept making Stacey do things—going into the pantry and getting things she was capable of hauling herself. Then Uncle Luther took Stacey on a tour of the house, starting with his study. Uncle Luther was especially proud of a wall of pictures of Luthers, and some falling-apart Bible kept under glass.

Miss Auntie told Cookie as they cleared the table, "You know what he's saying in there: 'You're taking *out* a good girl, you bring *back* a good girl.'"

"He wouldn't, Mama!"

"You know he would."

Watching those big women giggling like girls made Gayle sick. Especially since no one asked Gayle for her comments or invited her to giggle—as if she wasn't capable of girlish laughter. They'd have nothing to giggle about if Gayle hadn't set things in motion. Waved Stacey over. Started Cookie and Stacey talking about things other than Luke Twelve. Miss Auntie pushed hospitality

113

too far, suggesting Cookie bring Stacey upstairs to meet Great. It was the only time Gayle felt urged to materialize from sulky invisibility to say, "Great's asleep."

Finally Uncle Luther came in and reminded Cookie that she had to be back early. Miss Auntie and Uncle Luther strolled out on the porch to see Cookie and Stacey off while Gayle remained behind the curtains with José on her hip. She rubbed José's fat leg and rocked from side to side, seeing the day come to an end through the curtain lace and Cookie leaving her.

⚘16⚘

Miss Auntie took Uncle Luther's hand, swinging it playfully. "Bring back any memories?" Gayle didn't hear her uncle's reply.

"Can't run this one off," Miss Auntie said. "You know he's the one."

"I know no such thing," Uncle Luther stated.

"He's the one," Miss Auntie teased.

Gayle left her aunt and uncle on the porch. They were making too big a deal about nothing. Cookie had turned the fruits of their late-night talks, hair-styling sessions, and wardrobe planning into a family event. Honest to God. Nobody ever made José's daddy or Troy sweat through Twenty Questions. It was better when Stacey Alexander was *their* business. Hers and Cookie's.

José was now heavy on her hip. He would fall asleep within minutes. Gayle put him in the high chair and stroked his curly ringlets. "Babies so nice when you just looking at them."

She put the linen napkins in the hamper and collected the flatware and dishes for washing. Next she brought José upstairs, changed his diaper, and gave him a bottle before putting him to bed. After this she checked on

Great, then returned to the kitchen to wash the dishes. And where was Cookie? At the movies.

She filled the sink with hot water and suds and wondered what Cookie and Stacey were talking about. What people actually did on dates. She had hung out with Troy and José's daddy. They had both bought her things. But they never took her out on an actual date. She was counting on Cookie to tell her everything, starting with how much money Stacey spent.

Miss Auntie stuck her head in, remarked what a fine evening it was, what a fine boy Stacey was, and more of the same. It wouldn't have been so annoying if she had kept it to one intrusion, but Miss Auntie was a constant bag of sighing, blowing back and forth through the kitchen, retelling the whole evening. She must have come into the kitchen at least four times. The last time she was carrying a book.

"They make such a picture," Auntie said about Cookie and Stacey.

"It's just a date. Yawl act like it's a big deal." Her voice was tight. She had had enough.

"Haven't you ever been in love, Gayle?"

"Where you think José came from? The pet shop?"

"Your mouth, Gayle Ann," Miss Auntie scolded, though Gayle knew she wasn't deeply offended. Miss Auntie sat down at the breakfast counter and said, "Come, sweetie. Would you like to hear a love story?"

Gayle didn't like the weight on that *sweetie*. It was much too heavy.

Gayle's response, a shrug, didn't matter. Miss Auntie was in the mood for storytelling. She made herself comfortable, propping her elbows on the counter. One after the other her loosened sandals dropped to the floor. "It's a typical love story," she reflected. "You know: Girl and boy in love. Girl's family not crazy about boy."

"So."

"So, against their families' wishes and against all good sense they eloped the Saturday following high school graduation. Come Sunday morning they showed up on the girl's doorstep and made their announcement. Well! Of course the girl's brother threw them out. He wouldn't even speak to his sister—she had broken his heart so. His strong opposition only sealed the newlyweds tight. They left home for good. Tried to make it out there. Except, life proved a trial and a struggle with no family to rely on. They only had each other."

"Real romantic," Gayle deadpanned.

Miss Auntie removed her elbows from the table ceremoniously. "Well, I'm glad you think so, because those two were your mother and father."

Gayle wanted to say, "So," regardless of the flood around her, but she couldn't. Miss Auntie seemed to know that.

"Sweetie pie," Miss Auntie said carefully, "I get the feeling you don't know your mother. If you did, you'd understand why you're here."

Miss Auntie place a high school yearbook on the counter. She opened it and pointed out Ruth Bell Gates in the glee club photo and in the gospel choir photo. She watched as Gayle's indifference turned to deep gazes, seeing a photo of Mama, Miss Auntie, and another girl posing over a microphone. Those matching full-length dresses. Gloves crawling up their elbows. Hair puffed up and piled dangerously high.

"Senior talent night . . . our tribute to the sixties," Miss Auntie reminisced, delighted that Gayle was interested. "Ruthie, Patty, and I made up the Bells. We took first prize."

"That's Mama?"

"Child, that was only the beginning," she said, pulling

117

Gayle into the story. "All those old groups you heard about had nothing on us. We were Motown bound. Hear me? Look at us. We made those dresses in sewing class. We didn't wear makeup. Christian girls didn't wear makeup back then. But, Lord, didn't we smack some gel in our hair! It was a while before we figured out the Supremes wore wigs.

"The world was ours and David Whitaker knew it. He'd been working hard to get us heard by record companies in Philly, New York, and even Detroit. But Luther wouldn't have it. To make matters worse, the congregation was up in arms over us crooning baby, baby, honey, honey. They went to the pastor to get us removed from the choir."

"What!"

"Um-hm," Miss Auntie said, maintaining a taut line on Gayle, whose eyes now shone with interest. "Ruthie was torn between Luther and David, singing gospel and recording pop. Meanwhile, things had already been decided for Patty and me. Our mothers yanked us out of the Bells so fast we never heard the ringing. Come Sunday we were in our choir robes clapping and singing 'Show this Sinner on Home.'

"It wasn't so clear for Ruthie. Being in love with David didn't help matters. He was always telling Ruthie she was up there with Mahalia Jackson, Shirley Caesar, and Aretha Franklin, and maybe that was so. Ruthie went right to the soul. Sister Ruth Bell could make a shouter out of the most siddity folk. And no one felt her power more than Luther. He planned to install her as his premier soloist when he took over his daddy's church. Luther had plans for Ruthie. He even had three suitable beaus from powerful ministry families lined up for Ruthie to pick from.

"I believe she broke his heart when she put all her

118

love and trust in David. Ruthie figured she and David would make it big and her brother would come around. Of course it never happened. When she needed Luther she wouldn't go to him. And Luther, being unbending, wouldn't put out no arms. I believe you Gateses invented stubborn."

"What happened?" Gayle asked. "She got out onstage in the big city and bombed?"

"*Bombed?* Now I know you've never heard your mother sing," Miss Auntie said. "Being a solid Christian boy, David was more trusting than he was sharp. Oh, he got Ruthie a contract in New York, all right, but there was something crooked about it. Ruthie was pregnant with Junior, and the record company wouldn't promote her until after she gave birth. Back then you didn't go flaunting your pregnancy, married or not. It just wasn't done. So the company used Ruthie's voice on the records and another woman's face and name. The money was always long in coming and the dealings a bit shady. David couldn't get Ruthie work singing elsewhere because she was still under contract. Money problems followed them, starting with income taxes. David said the record company had promised to take out taxes when they signed the contract, but he couldn't prove it. Meanwhile Ruthie miscarried twice before having you. Year after you were born David was struck down with tuberculosis and a long bout of pneumonia, which left Ruthie to struggle with the hospital bills. Then there were the funeral costs. David's brothers—praise God—came through, but Ruthie had to release his body to them for burial back home. Loving David so, I know that must have broken her. But she wouldn't come home, and Luther wouldn't ask her. I don't think Ruth Bell forgave her brother for being so unbending or God for showing no mercy, and I believe that's why Ruth Bell refuses to lift her God-given voice."

Gayle was exhausted by the story. She didn't want to understand Mama, because understanding would loosen the grip on her heart.

"Miss Auntie, you s'posed to be Mama best friend, right? How come you couldn't do nothing?"

"I had done too much," Miss Auntie said. "That was the problem. I thought it was romantic, helping Ruthie sneak out to be with David. I encouraged her to follow her dreams instead of telling her to calm down and think things out. Ruthie had two gospel scholarships, you know. One from Fisk, another from Spelman. Instead of helping her make peace with her brother, I did her hair, helped sew her dress, and drove her to the train station to meet David. A real friend would not have let her ruin her life. A real friend would have told her to go home."

"And that's why you talked Uncle Luther into taking me and José in. 'Cause you feel guilty?"

"Yes," Miss Auntie admitted. "That has something to do with it. But mostly because Ruthie belongs here. This house needs her. Luther needs her. I need her. We've been like sisters all our lives and I miss her. If I can bring her home piece by piece I will."

Gayle sucked her teeth. "Mama ain't gonna leave our house in New York. 'Sides, being here's taught me a thing or two. It'll be different when I get back home. I'll help Mama out more."

Miss Auntie squeezed Gayle's hand. Her eyes bled pity.

Gayle snatched her hand back. "This ain't my home. I ain't staying in this dead place. I ain't playing slave girl while Cookie be the princess. Not hardly. I'm going home to Mama house soon's my money get straight."

Miss Auntie didn't even bother to assuage Gayle with

"sweetie pies." She rose and left Gayle alone. The book was still there, wide open, calling Gayle to search for Mama in its glossy pages. She had no intention of doing that. Mama wasn't plastered in that yearbook. Mama was home soaking her corns in their little house on Souf Road.

❧*17*❧

"THAT'S ALL yawl did? Drove down Weems Pond and looked at ripples in the water?" Gayle shook her head. "Just stop, Cookie. Stop right there. I don't want to hear no more."

Cookie flashed Gayle a toothy grin, got up, and closed her bedroom door.

"Can I trust you?"

Gayle gasped, excited. "What? Yawl did it? How was it? I bet Stacey gentle. He looks at you like you some piece of china could break. Go'n girl. I knew you had it in you. Now we gotta keep him coming back for more."

"Slow down, Gayle. We didn't do it."

Gayle sucked her teeth, utterly disappointed.

"But," Cookie said, not wanting to lose Gayle completely, "something's bound to happen."

"All right!" Gayle shouted, raising her hand, which Cookie slapped. They moved in closer to talk.

"Last night at the pond, we started talking about, you know, being attracted to each other."

"Uh-huh."

"And how when he first saw me—he described everything I wore!"

"Those kneesocks?"

"He said they were cute."

"Guy talk for 'I want some.'"

"No, no, no. He remembered them down to the color."

"Okay, okay. 'Nuff socks. Then what?"

"He pulled me close to him and was caressing my arms. I can't tell you how crazy that made me."

"Arms?"

"And rubbing my back."

"Um-hm, um-hm."

"And talking all that good talk and kissing my neck. Stacey's lips so soft and sweet, not too wet but just right, you know?"

"Yup, uh-huh."

"And he held me tight and I felt ... I felt his ... him."

"You felt his rod?" Gayle blurted out. "Bet Stacey hung like Donkey Kong. What next?"

"Keep your voice down." Cookie's eyes raced to the door, expecting to see her father. Her cheeks plummed. She couldn't talk. Not freely like Gayle.

Gayle missed girlfriend talking. She needed it and couldn't see what was holding Cookie back.

"Well?"

"That's it. Nothing happened," she said unconvincingly. "I mean, it could have. If Stacey said, Let's go to my dorm, I would have gone."

"Dag, Cookie. You sixteen, right? Overdue if you ask me."

Cookie opened her mouth to disagree, an automatic reaction, then closed it. She was making that clicking sound deep in her throat. Gayle nudged her to make her stop.

"I can't help it. I'm nervous."

"Nervous?"

"Look, Cousin. I know you don't understand how I feel—you not being saved—"

"Scuse my unsaved ass."

"See what I mean? Now, if you were saved you'd know I'm fighting a war inside. You'd know why I can't just let go."

"You're right, Cuz. I don't understand. You got some college dude puppy-dogging you, taking you places, treating you like gold, and you won't do your part 'cause you saved? Least tell me you scared of getting bit by AIDS or you scared of getting caught. Saved? Saved? What's that?"

"If you were saved you'd know. I'm in too deep and you can't help me. You don't understand."

"Try me."

Cookie searched Gayle's face. She collected herself. "Last Sunday in church. Remember 'Nearer to Thee' and how I was getting into it?"

"Who could forget? Brought the house down. Only wish Great could have been there."

"Well, before I sing, I get peaceful inside, you know? Peaceful like a still pond. When the organ is playing and the choir is moaning, a feeling comes over me. You know that goose-pimply feeling that crawls over you for no reason at all and makes you turn around to see who's there? Well, I know who's there. It's the Holy Ghost. And I don't try to control it. I just let it take over. I get filled with the Holy Ghost and I sing."

Cookie was now aware of Gayle's eyes, suspicious, squinting, unable to follow.

"Well, last Sunday ... last Sunday I wasn't filled with the Holy Ghost. I was singing because I knew Stacey was out there. I closed my eyes and heard his voice telling me to go on."

Gayle stared blankly, put off by the melodrama. She was waiting to hear some life-and-death dilemma. Not about some Holy Ghost.

"I'm in trouble," Cookie said. "I don't even know myself anymore."

"Cuz, you in love. That ain't trouble."

Cookie mouthed, "No," certain now more than ever that Gayle couldn't understand. She grabbed her pillow and pressed it against her stomach.

"So what you gonna do?" Gayle asked.

Cookie squeezed the pillow. "Talk to Mama."

Gayle stared Cookie down. "Do your ears know what your mouth just said? I can hear Miss Auntie now: 'Sweetie pie, hoes don't go to heaven, so glue your business shut till you get married.'"

Ordinarily that would have been worth a chuckle, but Cookie just sat hunched over the pillow, biting her nails.

"See, Cookie, you get me sick. Why you gotta drag your mother in on this?"

"Mama's okay," Cookie assured her. "I can tell her anything."

"You believe that?"

Cookie nodded.

"Talk to me," Gayle pleaded. "I'll tell you what you need to know."

"Mama will help me think things out."

"Think things out? You need to stop thinking so hard and go while it's flowing."

Cookie smiled wryly. "You *would* say that. Don't you ever think what your life would be like if you never had a baby?"

"Life without my baby? No!" Gayle cried. "He's my world."

"I meant, you'd still have your life ahead of you to

finish school, go to college, meet someone really nice, travel."

Gayle threw back her head and laughed, relieved the tension was now broken by Cookie's silliness. "Cookie, stop watching those commercials! If I didn't have José I wouldn't be thinking 'bout no college or sailing 'cross the seven seas. And for meeting someone 'nice.' I'd rather smell a guy coming than get tripped up by a 'nice' game."

Cookie wasn't listening. Gayle could see that. Her head was in the pillow and she was humming, as if to block Gayle out.

"So you going to tell Miss Auntie you all hot in the butt."

Cookie tapped Gayle's leg.

"You get me sick, Cookie. Tell, why doncha."

At least Miss Great was in a mood for talking and wanted some recipe. After she had her fill she passed the mason jar to Gayle. "Go 'head. Sip. It'll wash that blue on out."

Gayle no longer wondered how Great knew things. She raised the jar to her lips and sipped.

"What's the matter, baby? Heart broke?"

Gayle sat up closer to Great. No one had ever broken her heart before. And it was Cookie of all people.

"Cookie get me sick, Miss Great. All she knows is Stacey. Wanna save on 'lectricity? Say 'Stacey' 'round Cookie and see if the house don't light up."

"All hot and stupid on love, is she?"

"That ain't even the worse part. I help get him for her and she throws me over 'cause I don't understand. I ain't saved. I think we getting closer and she leaves me behind."

"Cookie ain't leave you. There's no leaving family."

"Mama left."

Great made a low grunt. "You here. The baby here. Right foot step, the left drag behind it."

"Mama ain't moving down Souf. That I know for sure."

Another grunt. "Better listen to what I know: Ruthie be here soon enough. . . ."

Gayle watched Great's eyelids flicker, then close. She returned the half-empty mason jar to its hiding place, then stood at the window nearest Great's bed to stare out past the gate. She didn't bother with the window on the opposite side of the room. She had no desire to gaze east at the patch of field where the crosses grew.

Voices came from below. Gayle looked down. Cookie and Miss Auntie stepped out from the porch and started toward the gate.

Miss Auntie gonna beat Cookie's butt good. Tear down one of those peach tree branches and switch Cookie's butt purple.

Gayle watched the hems of their skirts dip left and right as they strolled lazily beyond the gate. Once off the property they removed their flats and continued barefoot, occasionally bumping hips from walking so close to each other. Miss Auntie put her arm around Cookie's neck, pretending to choke her daughter, and Cookie screamed "Mommmeeee!" loud and silly. They separated and came together before disappearing into the woods, taking their mother-daughter talk with them.

❧ 18 ❧

Gayle licked another envelope, confident that her girls would write back. So what if the only letters that had arrived up until now were penned in Mama's heavy-handed scrawl. Terri and Lynda could not be blamed if booming rhythms under the August sun forced them out into the streets day and night. At least Lynda and Terri had the decency to lose track of her from a thousand miles away. They hadn't forgotten her to her face like some so-called sister-cousin who was never there.

That's why Cookie could never be down like a home-girl. Instead of being tight with Gayle, Cookie let people come between them. First it was the Lord. Then Stacey. And when they talked about sex, something Gayle could contribute her full knowledge to, Cookie went running to her mother, of all people.

If it weren't for the iffy promise of driving lessons, Gayle wouldn't have bothered to pack up José to tag along with Cookie for choir practice.

" 'Bout those driving lessons," Gayle brought up as they drove into town. "I know yawl southerners born with a steering wheel in your hands, so while I'm here might as well get with the customs. I got the basics down pat: seat belts on, start 'er up, check the mirror, throw it in drive, vroom. Just take me to an open lot or some back road."

Cookie's "maybe later" made Gayle fold her arms and pop her gum. It sounded like no to her.

Cookie apologized. "I'm just so nervous," she explained. "I haven't seen Stacey since the pond and we have to talk. Take it slow. Last night Mama said, Be in control of yourself, Be in control of your life. Mama said sex will weigh a young body down or stop it cold—and I know she's right, but when I'm with Stacey I don't hear any of that." She shook her head in a moment of happy indecision. "If I don't talk to him I won't be able to concentrate tonight, and I can't mess up this rehearsal. It's so important."

Control? Was that the best Miss Auntie could do for Cookie? Tell her to control herself? Gayle coughed to keep from laughing. And to think her heart had been bruised watching Cookie and Miss Auntie disappear off into the woods talking their mother-daughter talk. She hadn't missed a thing.

"It's only choir practice, Cookie. The way you be wailing those solos Sunday, you don't have a thing to worry about."

Cookie told Gayle she wouldn't be singing any solos this Sunday. Uncle Luther had invited Pastor Samuels, a divinity school chum, to come up from Atlanta and preach. And Pastor Samuels was bringing Sister Rebecca Lloyd as a guest soloist.

"You know Sister Rebecca Lloyd," Cookie insisted. "I know you do. They always play her on the radio."

Gayle rolled her eyes and popped her gum while Cookie listed Rebecca Lloyd's biggest hits.

"If Sunday's s'posed to be so important, when we

picking up my dress?" Gayle asked. "Or am I going as the family charity case?"

"Maybe tomorrow."

"Maybe tomorrow?"

"Ask Mama if she can take you. I think tomorrow Stacey and I—"

Gayle tossed her head, not wanting to hear any more. "You get me sick, Cookie. Ain't you s'posed to be controlling yourself?"

As expected, Stacey guarded the door of the recreation room, anticipating Cookie's arrival. As rude as he pleased, he said some kind of "hi" and dragged Cookie off to the garden before Gayle could finish talking. There was nothing Stacey had to say that could not have waited—at least from what Gayle could see standing at the door, rocking José so he wouldn't cry out. By the pleading hands, it looked like he was apologizing. From her swaying, it looked like she was going for it. When the couple entered the recreation room, Cookie was flushed with relief. She left Stacey to join the other churchies in their talk of Sister Rebecca Lloyd, who was such a professional she didn't have to attend rehearsal, but instead faxed a few sheets of music, which all the churchies wanted to see for themselves.

With José in her arms, Gayle slid over to be near Stacey. He didn't notice. He hadn't removed his gaze from Cookie.

Dog. They in love like in the movies. All make-believe and starry eyed. Stacey probably stirs soup with Cookie in the soup kitchen just to get next to her perfume. Cookie ain't even give him the main thing and he so full of her.

Stacey finally acknowledged Gayle so he could pour out his devotion to "Constance." "Did you hear that? The girl is truly blessed. She's the sole reason I wake up early on Sunday. I mean, Sunday won't be Sunday without Constance's solo."

It was after the fifth praise of Constance that Gayle said, "Yo. Don't butter me, slick. I ain't the one whose drawers you want to drop."

The choir, with all eyes on their director, missed the drama. They didn't see Stacey's head jerk right, his complexion darken, or his eyes cut daggers into Gayle.

When she happened to look up, all Cookie saw was Stacey Alexander tearing off, marching out the door.

"I just wanted him to shut up," Gayle told José. "But this'll do."

The final chord of "I Am a Witness" was still resounding in the air when Cookie ran to Gayle to learn why Stacey had left. Gayle strained to recall the conversation word for word.

"Something 'bout waking up on Sundays to hear you sing in church."

Cookie refused to believe, so Gayle raised one hand in testimony. "I only know what he said: 'It won't be the same without Constance singing lead.'"

Cookie paused, rolling the thought around.

"He might not even show to church."

"What?"

"'Sunday won't be Sunday without Constance's solo,'" Gayle said carefully, mocking Stacey's intonation.

"Noooo," Cookie sang, wanting to be pulled in the opposite direction.

"You know, he's right," Gayle obliged. "Now, personally, when that Sister Lloyd starts crowing your solo I'm gon' be with everyone else: 'Yeah, that's nice, but you ain't Cookie.'"

"Get out of here, Cousin." She fluttered her lashes coyly.

"And who does she think she is, faxing her sheet music

instead of rehearsing with yawl. That's rude," Gayle preached.

Cookie rushed to Sister Lloyd's defense. "This very moment Sister Lloyd is singing at a big revival down in New Orleans. We're lucky to have her on Sunday."

"Lucky? She the lucky one—got everyone kissing her toes," Gayle said. " 'Member my friend Joycie who danced the African queen in this show? Joycie had the crowd stomping and cheering. Well, her group did a spring show with another girl dancing the lead. People clapped, but it was thin and polite clapping, and that other girl was crushed with a capital ouch."

Cookie waved Gayle on. "Sister Lloyd is the queen of standing ovations. She'll bring the house down all by herself."

"Folks'll be polite—'cause that's how yawl are. But they won't give her that real amen." Gayle paused to let Cookie consider it all, then added, "Now, if you helped her out some, she'd get it."

"Just stop it, Cuz. Just stop. Sister Lloyd don't need my help."

"Guess not," Gayle said. "Don't know why I care so much. But you saw, Stacey didn't even stick around."

The house was abuzz with preparations. Miss Auntie couldn't decide between making dinner reservations in town or having the Samuelses and Sister Lloyd over to the house. She finally decreed it inhospitable and unforgivable to send her guests out, and began preparing a menu. Even Uncle Luther was remarkably light with anticipation, talking about divinity school days, laughing with Miss Auntie at the dinner table. Cookie was somewhat moody, waiting for a phone call from Stacey, which never came. However, once Sister Lloyd's name was mentioned, Cookie joined in her parents' enthusiasm, telling Auntie and Uncle how Sister Lloyd had faxed sheet music in for the rehearsal. Uncle Luther told Cookie, "You all make Sister Lloyd feel at home. She's on the road quite a bit."

Cookie kissed her daddy on the cheek and reassured him she would do just that.

❧ 19 ❧

Joy RINGED the grounds where Freedom Gate stood ready
to receive worshipers. Gayle held José tightly and dragged
her feet behind Miss Auntie. While everyone called out
praises and greetings and waved to one another, Gayle
sealed her lips so that "um-hm" was the only utterance
she could make. She had no intention of losing herself in
the Holy Ghost, who was swooping about and sopping up
all the high-spirited folks. After all, no one had bothered
to take her shopping for a dress. In fact, her aunt, uncle,
and cousin had all forgotten her in their excitement over
the visitors. Cookie's concerns were wrapped around Stacey Alexander and if he would call and what she'd do to
make things right. Miss Auntie had very few "sweetie
pies" to dole out and even fewer wisdoms that generally
followed the "sweetie pies." Even Uncle Luther ignored
her. He stopped darkening the house with his tight, joyless face and didn't made that *click-click* sound at the
sight of Gayle and her child.

As they entered the vestibule, Gayle was aware that
Miss Auntie had for the first Sunday that she could recall
failed to point out some historical detail about Freedom
Gate. How the church got its name. When the first brick

was laid. How the stump was transplanted from the fields. Where the Civil Rights meetings were held. How Ruth Bell led the choir. What Uncle Luther's first sermon was about.

Miss Auntie was too busy donning her First Lady of the Church face. She did exchange pleasantries with the choirmaster, who was giving final instructions to the choir as they lined up for the procession, but kept it brief, taking pity on him because of his preoccupation with Sister Lloyd's arrival.

Cookie didn't even look their way because Cookie, in her blue satin robe, was in thick with her heaven-bound friends, who were caught up in the excitement. A soprano had spotted Sister Lloyd being ushered into the pastor's chamber. They tugged on one another's robes and whispered, "She's here, she's here."

When Gayle turned to ignore her cousin, she saw Stacey Alexander enter through the side door with a friend—a football teammate, judging by his height and size. Stacey led his friend to a pew as near to the choir chamber as possible. He then excused himself and made his way over to Miss Auntie as she and Gayle continued up the aisle to the first row. As Miss Auntie spoke to another church member, Stacey stood at attention, waiting for Miss Auntie to finish inquiring about the woman's family. Gayle pushed out her hip and tapped her toe, feeling Stacey deliberately ignore her. She had to smack José's hand to stop him from cooing and reaching out to Stacey.

"Why Stacey, sweetie, please join us," Miss Auntie said with a painted smile. Gayle hated that face on Miss Auntie.

Stacey thanked her but declined, explaining that he had brought his roommate. Miss Auntie wouldn't take no for an answer and tried to persuade Stacey to have his roommate join them, but Stacey said he couldn't do that and apologized for "the intrusion." He and Miss Auntie played out one more round of she offering and he respectfully refusing before Stacey excused himself to join his roommate.

"Did you catch that, Miss Auntie? He liked to kill hisself not to look my way, let alone not speak. It ain't really 'bout no roommate."

"I can't imagine Stacey being rude, unless you gave him reason," Miss Auntie said as they were taking their seats. "The truth is, Stacey is a well-trained boy. He knows this pew is reserved for family and special guests. Sitting here would be like making an announcement, almost bragging—and Luther would not appreciate that."

"Then why'd you invite him to sit with us?" Gayle asked.

Rather than respond, Miss Auntie turned to acknowledge another church member.

Um-hm, Gayle thought. People take being nice too far, saying and doing things they don't mean. Then it's your hard luck when you believe them. Like driving lessons, buying dresses, being sisters, being family. People should say what they mean and be who they are.

"Can I get an amen on that?" she whispered to José, patting his chubby hands together.

As the choir sang the processional hymn, the choir members, the deacons, and the two pastors marched to their designated stations. It was a beautiful sight. Sunlight poured through the great windows overlooking the front, shining down on the satiny blue of the choir robes, the potted lilies on the altar, the twin velvet thrones where Reverends Gates and Samuels sat poised for nothing

136

short of glory. Then, in the final phrases of the processional, Sister Rebecca Lloyd appeared from the pastor's chambers and took her place at the head of the choir, where the sunlight favored her and all of her lavender.

The service went on nicely. Uncle Luther worked up his congregation, then handed them over to Pastor Samuels, who regaled them with anecdotes of divinity school days. From there he went into the heart of the sermon. The same preacher who made folks chuckle made them go um, um, um.

Gayle wasn't moved. Gayle chewed her gum.

Upon the choirmaster's nod, the choir rose in unison. Sister Lloyd also rose, but in her own sweet time. Once on her feet, Sister Lloyd proceeded to take over. Even the choirmaster got out of her way. Sister Lloyd spoke a silent language with her head tilting so that her hat feather talked. Glory seeped out of that short but grand woman, and people waved their hankies to catch it. She hadn't even hummed a full string and people were falling out. Uncle Luther beamed, filled with the joy it gave him to sit back and show off his church.

Gayle chewed and chewed, with eyes fixed on Cookie. *Would she? Would she do it for Stacey?*

The choir obeyed the choirmaster, whose batonlike hands said, "Give her room, give her room." They prepared a background harmony that was so soft, so perfect, Sister Lloyd floated above it.

Although Cookie had once sung "I Am a Witness," in Sister Lloyd's interpretation the hymn spoke new meaning. Her voice knew firsthand the twists of the winding road as well as the promise of sweetness at journey's end. Those who witnessed instantly became her people and called out to her, "I'm on that road with you!"

Gayle chewed furiously. She saw Cookie's eyes close

as Cookie stepped forth from the body of blue satin. She heard Cookie's mezzo-soprano climb and linger upon the crest of Sister Lloyd's rolling contralto. Except for a momentary lapse—detectable only to someone looking for it—Sister Lloyd pressed on, completely unruffled. She had been there before and was able to answer. Sister Lloyd reached down and pulled from her lower drawer— yes she did!—thunder, circled with lightning—yes she did!—and hurled it at the interloper, knocking her down, down, down. With hat feather talking that talk, she snatched back her solo and made it all sound rehearsed that way—she was good, you know!

Suddenly Cookie found herself disgraced and standing apart from the choir. There was nowhere to turn in the faces that surrounded her. Her mother's face stood out high and reproachful above all others. Her father's shame and disappointment were masked by his hand. She searched and searched but couldn't find Stacey Alexander through her puddled eyes.

Now satisfied, Gayle removed her gum.

When the service ended Cookie ran straight for her father, but he would not speak to her. She went running to Sister Lloyd and made apologies spill out like rain. Sister Lloyd said, "Darling, we all get caught up in the spirit." She was so gracious, she knocked Cookie down for the second time, as the hat feather danced.

Stacey tried to break through the droves of worshipers to comfort Cookie, but Miss Auntie interceded and told him it was best that he didn't see Cookie just now. Gayle flashed her teeth at Stacey. It was all so funny.

When they got home Uncle Luther ordered Cookie into the study. Gayle tried to stand outside the door, but Miss Auntie wouldn't have it.

"I don't see what the fuss is about," Gayle said innocently. "All she did was harmonize with Sister Lloyd."

For a change, Miss Auntie didn't drip sweetness. She looked tight. "Gayle Ann, you can't begin to understand the seriousness of Cookie's behavior. She embarrassed her father, made the choirmaster look a fool, and was simply rude to Sister Lloyd, and what's more, she allowed herself to succumb to pride. And that's one sin the saved dare not fall to."

The more Miss Auntie went on to explain the fall of Lucifer, the less sense Gayle could make of what all that had to do with Cookie's horning in on Sister Lloyd's solo. Miss Auntie saw this in the blank eyes and the gum chewing and told Gayle to bring the baby upstairs and to have Miss Foster come down to the kitchen.

Gayle was slow taking José upstairs. She was afraid all the fireworks would become stifled in the big house. But Uncle Luther's voice proved big enough. Midway up the stairs, Gayle heard Uncle Luther thundering pride and fall and Cookie crying as though the world had come to an end.

❧20❧

GAYLE took the clothespin from between her teeth and snapped it on the line. She stood barefoot on top of the stool, enjoying the sky and the leafy trees that seemed to wave at her and filled the air with the smell of overripe peaches. It was wonderful. Almost as wonderful and filling as the spoiled sweetness of having Cookie all to herself.

If Gayle wanted to, she could suggest to her uncle that it wasn't really Cookie's fault. Cookie had been overwhelmed by that Stacey dude telling her her voice was better than Sister Lloyd's. Cookie probably saw Stacey out in the pews while she was singing and forgot herself. Sparks would really jump then. Uncle Luther would end that Stacey thing once and for all.

Cookie would be past her kneesocks in misery, and Gayle knew about misery. They could wade in it together, trashing everybody, especially Stacey for starting up this mess, then Uncle Luther, and Miss Auntie, and Mama and Junie and Troy and Troy Mama, and the homegirls for not writing. Trash everybody. She and Cookie could plan their escape to New York in Cookie's car.

Gayle stared off into the waving trees, imagining herself and Cookie sailing along the highway, the radio broadcasting their freedom. She saw herself behind the wheel and heard Cookie telling her to slow down as she prepared to make a wide turn. Before she completely rounded the turn, the very real growl of an engine cut into her daydream. She glanced over her shoulder and caught a glimpse of Stacey pulling into the driveway. His car door slammed. Gayle went on hanging linen napkins as his figure grew in the corner of her eye. She armed herself with indifference.

Stacey reached down into the hamper and lifted José. "Tell Constance I'm here."

Gayle scouted left, then right, and went back to pinning napkins. "Must be the wind shaking up the leaves 'cause I sho' don't see no one."

He sighed heavily. "Just tell her I'm here."

"Is my name Hazel? Do I look like a maid? How you gon' order me around . . . didn't even speak on Sunday?"

"I had nothing to say to you Sunday."

"Well scuse me, your rudeness. I ain't talking about no full-out conversation. Just the common courtesy of saying hi. You stand there in church looking 'bove my head like you got a crick in your neck."

"Look. I don't appreciate you flapping that hole on the side of your face talking about dropping drawers. Especially where Constance is concerned."

"Ooh, Stacey. I'm trembling."

He bent down to put José back in the hamper. "Just tell her I'm here."

"She don't want to see you."

"Says who? Tell her to come down."

"And I told you, my name ain't Hazel."

"All right, all right," he said, shifting his whole manner. "Would you *please* tell Constance to come down."

"Don't you see I'm busy?" She didn't care if he caught her grinning. It was funny.

He offered to hang her laundry and watch the baby while she went upstairs. This was precisely the reason she couldn't stand him. Dudley-Do-Right-Black-Knight-on-a-White-Mustang-Storming-the-Tower-to-Save-the-Princess.

Gayle jumped off the stool.

Everybody knocking themselves out to save Cookie. Ain't no one trying to save me.

"Just do me this one favor," he added.

He was making her sick with all that life-and-death begging. She sashayed over to the screen door, stuck her head inside, and yelled, "Yo, Cook, Stacey down here to see you," loudly enough to draw Uncle Luther from his study. Stacey threw his hands up.

As she hoped, Uncle Luther stepped outside, thumbs hooked in belt loops, to have a few words with Stacey Alexander. Gayle tried to listen but Uncle Luther kept whatever he had to say between him and the Black Knight, who was now reduced to nodding respectfully. Cookie made it downstairs in time to see her father entering the kitchen and Stacey driving away. She ran out to the gate, then back inside the kitchen.

Gayle stood nearby, hoping to catch whatever sifted through the screen door. Cookie was naive enough to ask her daddy what her boyfriend wanted. Uncle Luther was too disgusted to answer. Gayle heard angry feet pounding up the stairs and a door slamming. Sounded like a Fourth of July special! The house was heating up good!

Then Miss Auntie's voice emerged. She was telling Uncle Luther, "A week's worth of punishment is enough."

Uncle Luther bordered on comic rage, ranting and pacing just like Mama did when Gayle or Junie went too far. "If you could have only heard your daughter. 'What did Stacey want?' Not 'Good afternoon, Daddy. Are you well,

Daddy,' but 'What did Stacey want?' I ask you, Ginny, is this the child we raised? Is it? No sir! That boy is not welcome here He has my daughter under a spell."

"Luther, she's in love. Keep on and you'll push her to do the wrong thing."

"Can't do nothing in her room."

"Love will find a way, Luther," Miss Auntie argued. Smothered talk followed, nothing Gayle could make out except for "Ruth Bell." That stopped her cold. She tried to hear better but all she could get was Ruth Bell, Ruth Bell, Ruth Bell, rising and falling in Miss Auntie's hushed tones. Uncle Luther had stopped ranting.

Gayle scooped up José, came inside the kitchen, and stole past her aunt and uncle. She had to race to Cookie's room before Miss Auntie came up there with her sweetie pies. Cookie didn't need all that sugar. She needed ugly. The kind Gayle could walk her through.

"Yo, Cook, let me in."

There was no answer, so Gayle turned the knob and entered. Cookie was lying facedown on the bed, her fingers dangling over the side.

"You ain't crying, is you?" Gayle came closer. "This ain't nothing to cry about. Stacey'll be back and if he don't, later for him."

Cookie swallowed a hard sob.

"You can't blame Stacey for cutting out. Uncle told him to stay away and you know Stacey big on respect. What you want? Him to slug it out with Uncle? Grow up, Cookie. That's in the movies."

Cookie mumbled that she didn't feel well and wanted to be left alone.

Gayle wasn't fooled. She knew that Cookie wanted her to speak up about Sister Lloyd. Tell everyone how she had planted that thought in Cookie's head.

Gayle ran the tip of her tongue along her chipped

tooth. She felt bad for Cookie, but not that bad. No one can make you do what you don't want. Not really. Deep down Cookie wanted to outsing Sister Lloyd and show off for Stacey. Everybody got some ugly in them no matter how saved they claim to be. Even Cookie.

"Stop crying, Cuz. You know I can't stand all that boo-hooing."

Cookie turned over so Gayle could see her tearstained face. "You don't know how I feel. You've never been in love. You've never watched someone you love walk away when you need them. You don't even have feelings." She rolled over and continued to cry.

Gayle stuck out the hip that carried her son. "Oh, yeah. My life's been Disney World. One long fun ride after another. A real scream, starting with the birthing table . . . no Mama, no Big José, nothing for the pain. It really got funny in the hospital when José finally showed up talking about adoption. Oh, and let's not forget Abortion Wonderland. I wonder where Troy went. I wonder why he ain't tried to find me. My grand prize? Being sold off into slavery to my corny-assed relatives. I've been toughing it out since day one and my eyes are still dry. Know why? 'Cause I'm a woman. Can't be crying about every little heartbreak."

"Maybe you should. Maybe you wouldn't be so hard and ugly. Now leave me alone. I want to cry."

"Fine," Gayle said. "Cry. Drown in it, why doncha." She slammed the door behind her. Anything to get away from all that crying. The last thing she wanted was to let go. Not with the flood she was carrying. Crying would only sharpen hurts she had pushed way back. And who wanted to feel all of that?

She dumped José into his crib, then turned her back to keep from looking at him. He filled his lungs and screamed, suddenly being out of her arms. Gayle went to the window, determined not to be moved. Her son, equally insistent, refused to give in and yelled with all his power to be picked up.

She turned, feeling the shadow of another body in her room. Her heart jumped, anticipating Cookie standing there with an apology, thick and soppy as she imagined it would be.

It was Uncle Luther. "What's all this hollering?"

Gayle folded her arms.

Uncle Luther took heavy steps to the fat little arms stretching up from the crib. He picked up José and started marching to the door.

"My baby!"

"Hush."

"He was only crying. I got him. I got him."

"Leave us men alone," Uncle Luther said.

Gayle stood on the top of the stairs watching José's head nestled in Uncle Luther's arms. She ran into Great's room.

"Miss Great, Miss Great, Uncle Luther took my baby."

"Um-hm."

"Miss Great, I said Uncle Luther took José. You know he hates us. What you think he gon' do?"

"Grabbed him out of your loving arms, did he?"

Gayle sucked her teeth.

"Don't worry about the baby. He's in the best hands he could be in," Great said. "What worry me is all that stir ain't boiled over."

Gayle moaned. *Cookie, Cookie. Everything's about Cookie.*

"They still mad at Cookie over that Sister Lloyd business. Won't let her boyfriend see her."

Great looked at Gayle. "I can't picture Cookie forgetting her place like that."

"Maybe her boyfriend put it in her head. Snaked it in

there, being all slick and sly. You know how boys are. Tell you anything to get you to lie down."

This was where Great was supposed to plant an "um-hm." Great just let Gayle go on talking, wrapping her tongue around herself.

"Feeling ugly?"

Gayle laid her head down next to her great-grandmother. She felt Great's fingers, long and coarse with age, caress her scalp, then her temples. She stuck her thumb in her mouth and thought, Mama used to do this—pat her hair and scratch her scalp.

"Maybe I'm a little sorry," she told Great. "But she hurt me like I ain't never been hurt before. I go thinking we're for real, like sisters looking out for each other. But as soon as Stacey jump in the picture she push me aside, so I had to pay her back. I thought she just gonna be standing up there with a big 'Oops!' on her face. And after church I was gonna say, 'So there,' and it would be payback between us. I didn't know the whole world gonna fall apart."

"Now listen, Miss Fresh Thing, and listen good. Bible says there's a time to put away your childishness and the time is now."

"I don't read the Bible, Miss Great. I don't know what you mean."

"You know 'zactly what I mean. Whatever mess you started with Cookie is done with. You have a bigger job 'head of you."

"What job?"

"I seen it in a dream 'fore you stomp on in here. Thought it was my time 'cause I could see the light. I was rejoicing, shaking off my burdens and my aches, and was marching to the light. I felt something godly grip my shoulders and stop me from marching. Before me stood a gate. Not forged with pearls like you picture for heaven but a plain gate like out the yard. It opened and the baby crawled through. Emanuel. Then before my eyes he rose into a man and swung the gate wide open and led the congregation through, showing them the way, preaching and baptizing and saying the praises of the Lord . . . with all them Luthers looking down on him. You know, Sonny still laughs full and loud in paradise. Then I woke up looking at you."

Gayle sat straight up. "Not my baby."

"Hush that, child. He's theirs as sure as you mine."

Gayle shook her head unh-unh.

"Got their face. Built strong like they built."

"Unh-unh."

"Lungs fill this house with the Word."

"That's just crying."

"And praising the Lord."

"He ain't growing up here. We going back home."

"Too late," Great pronounced. "If my eyes seen it, it's true."

Not wanting to hear Miss Great's prophecy, Gayle turned to the laughter coming from outside. She hurried to the window but couldn't see straight down, as the terrace blocked her view. All she knew was that Uncle Luther was out on the porch making her son laugh.

❧ 21 ❧

"C'MON, COOKIE. We can still catch that fellowship meeting if we hurry."

Gayle turned the knob. She entered the shade-drawn room and found Cookie lying facedown on her pillow, worn out from yet another day of crying. The sandwich Gayle had brought up earlier sat on the nightstand minus a bite.

Cookie was letting her heartbreak take over. She had stopped going to the soup kitchen to stir soup, and she had missed two choir rehearsals. Gayle missed the rides into town, stopping off at the Dairy Queen, the mile-high cakes, the singing at rehearsals. It wasn't a stroll on the Avenue back home, but it was being out with Cookie. And the baby.

Gayle tapped her foot. "I know you feel me here."

Cookie refused to turn over, let alone twitch.

"You just gonna lie there?"

Cookie wouldn't budge. She had turned off Gayle just as she had everyone in the house.

"Dog, Cookie. I thought we were supposed to be like sisters looking out for each other. But no. You go tossing me to the curb like a broken toy 'cause someone else

come along. That's not how you do someone you ..."
love? I ain't saying that. "Look. You hurt my feelings,
Cookie. I had to get you back. Let you know I'm still
here. Now, don't 'spect me to go 'nouncing to the world
'bout Sister Lloyd, but I'll say it to you: I'm sorry. Okay?
I said, I'm sorry."

Nothing.

"Fine." Gayle grabbed the plate and turned on her
heel. "Just fine, Cookie."

Miss Auntie sat in the kitchen flipping through
index cards to prepare for a seminar at the college. If it
weren't for the prospect of being walled in by educated
black folks talking over her head about history, Gayle
would pack up José and sit through it just to get out of
the house.

"Sure you won't join us? You just might learn something."

"Nah," she said in place of the smart retorts that
occurred to her.

From nowhere a chill swept through her. She rubbed
her arms, dotted with goose pimples. "Don't you feel
that?"

"Feel what, sweetie?" she asked, her thoughts elsewhere.

"The house. All creepy and quiet."

Miss Auntie smiled without looking up from her
cards. "Not exactly New York City, is it?"

Gayle shook her head. "It ain't that." It was a quiet
Great talked about. How the house missed Sonny's big
laugh and the music his wife loved and Mama's singing—none of which Gayle had ever heard, but which
she missed all the same. It had been weeks since
Cookie had erupted with something cheery, loud, and
stupid about her Jesus or her Stacey. Even Miss Auntie

149

was not inspired to say southern things at the dinner table. And Uncle Luther seemed to have lost all will to hurl thunder at the least provocation. It was as if the stillness among the planted crosses had spread up the walk and inside the house, lulling everyone into silence. That is, except for José, who was always full of life.

Gayle locked up after Uncle Luther and Miss Auntie left for the evening. She stood outside Cookie's door and tapped lightly. Only talking and hearing talk would kill the emptiness in the house. Talking had healing power. Both she and Cookie would feel better if they talked. She knocked harder.

"See, Cookie. We could be making french fries and playing our tapes on the stereo."

Still no answer.

She went down the hall to Great's room. Great was on one of her journeys. She could tell. It was the calm of a face that smiled from inside. Miss Great just wanted to die! She seemed so happy.

Gayle sat down on the bed and rubbed Great's arm gently to pull her back. She didn't care if Great woke up cranky—not when she so desperately needed to talk.

"You hungry, Miss Great? I can warm up that broth you like."

Great said she wasn't hungry but she would like some recipe. Gayle hesitated, but Great fussed and got her way. Gayle brought out the mason jar from the bottom dresser drawer. It had thickened into a funky brown color on the bottom, leaving a deep orange on the top.

"Miss Great, don't you get tired of lying in that bed? Wouldn't you like to sit by the window? We could catch the sunset. It ain't color TV, but it's a picture. Let's go sit by the window."

"Sun sets west, dudn't it?"

Gayle didn't really know and just said, "Uh-huh."

"Naw, naw. Don't want to see the sun. Hurts what's left of my eyes. I wants to sit east," Great said.

Gayle figured it out. East overlooked the crosses and the hills. "We gon' miss our sunset," she whined.

"Sit me east," Great snapped.

Gayle grumbled but helped Great into her wheelchair all the same. Great was much lighter than the first time Gayle had lifted her.

"Now, sweetie," Great said. "Something I want you to do for me. Old folks not supposed to see their reflection. Scares 'em into a heart attack. Go on and cover my bureau mirror with a sheet. Then take all them pictures with shiny glass and face 'em down."

Gayle wrinkled her nose. "Miss Great, that don't sound right."

"Didn't ask you what sound right."

Gayle did as she was told, although hesitation pulled on every step. First she turned all the pictures of family facedown on the bureau. The sheet thing made her question her own good sense. Great was so intent on having her way that Gayle went along, taking a sheet from the linen closet. She stood on a chair and hung the sheet over the mirror. Then and only then would her great-grandmother consent to being wheeled across the room and transferred to the rocker. In return Great was full of praises for Gayle's helping her over to the window.

Gayle retrieved the mason jar and undid the clamp on the lid.

"Let's have a taste," Great said, impatient.

Gayle tilted the jar with care, allowing Great to

catch her breath between sips. She waited for her great-grandmother to say if the recipe had been made correctly and if it was on the second change. Great never did. Instead she asked for another sip and told Gayle to take a sip, calling it the "libation." Then, without any help from Gayle, Miss Great set the rocker in motion.

Great was saying something, but what? Her lips moved, but no sound came out.

"What's that, Miss Great?"

"... It came from Mbeke, torn from her sister, Who told her child Mahalia, Who stole the paper with Mbeke's slave price, Who told her Mahalia that ope'd the gate and gave us our name, Who told her son Luther who like his pa preached in the field. Who told his son Luther that build Freedom Gate to set us free, Who told his wife Abigail that gave her only gat[1] son to the world, Who telling you that you do the same."

"Stop that, Miss Great. You Telling, ain't you?"

"It came from Mbeke, torn from her sister ..."

Gayle covered her ears. "I ain't listening."

As Great spoke, the swing of her rocking chair aided her cadence. "All them Luthers preached the Word, for the Truth is in the Word and the Word set you free. Yes. All them Luthers preached the Word, and all them Mahalias blessed with voice. Come from snatching out we Wolf[2] tongue. All them Mahalias blessed with voice.

"What 'they' calls the Cotton Song be the Calling Up Song. Women sing, pick cotton, call up children long gone away, call up kinfolk long gone away.

[1] begotten
[2] The word *Wolof*, an African dialect, has been changed through the retelling of the family history.

"Mbeke sang the Calling Up with her baby, Mahalia, 'longside her, sang how they was gals in the homeland, gathering cow[3] shells by the water—"

She knew! She knew! "That shell tied up there in the hanky?"

But Great could not be stopped. "—she sang 'bout getting kotched off the land, thrown into the whale's belly, and how they lost their Wolf tongue in the journey, and drummed thoughts to each other like this"—and she made that throat-locking sound, the sound Uncle Luther and Cookie made when words would not do.

"When the whale spit them out onto land, Mbeke got torn from her sister. But Mbeke kept one cow shell in her fist and her sister kept the other.

"Now, time turned and passed when Mbeke, who they called Becky, Ma Becky, and Singing Becky, gat eight babies. All long gone sold away—to Massa's wife people in Car'lina and Virginny, all but the baby girl, Mahalia. And Mbeke told Mahalia 'bout getting kotched, and how to spot the first cotton bloom, and how to make healings from what grows, and how to Call Up the lost ones, and not to lay cross eyes on the Guinea[4] woman 'cause she could be kin, long gone away.

"Now, Mahalia snatched the paper from Massa book. Took the lash on the back and lived to tell her own Mahalia how she snatch Ma Becky's slave price from Massa book, and how to fix healings, how to Call Up the lost ones, and be careful who you cross eyes at, 'cause she could be your kin, long gone away.

"Time turned and passed when Mahalia's Mahalia

___

[3] cowrie shells
[4] African

swung ope' the gate out front, let the Union soldiers ride in. And when the cap'n fix to spear Massa baby boy, Mahalia snatch up the chile and runned with it out the gate, in the woods. Some say runned and some say flied. But that Mahalia ope'd the gate, gave us our name. And some of her brothers went last we knowed to Canada. One brother went last we knowed to Ohio.

"It was Mahalia's son Luther who preached the Word like his pa, also called Luther. They'd all named Luther 'cause you can find your way home if you knows your name.

"Now, Mahalia's Luther couldn't read at all, but could see through God's eyes: Told how freed Nigroes gon' build a church as fine as any and told how he wouldn't live to preach from its pulpit, but his son and grandson would.

"He was buried by his own son Luther, who read, I say *read*, psalms over his grave, being the first to preach from a book. Hallelujah! And that Luther got to be an old man and a widower, then lost all his children to the pox. Married him a spry gal, Miss Abigail Coston, what gave him a giant for a son. Another Luther, we calls Sonny. And when that Luther came of age together they built Freedom Gate.

"Now Sonny 'tended college, and was a marching preacher in the Civil Rights with folk gathered 'round and 'round to hear the Word. He was a tall-standing man, couldn't play boy to save his life. Sonny's firstborn, also Luther, preached the Word with fire, and his baby girl Ruth Bell got the Calling Up voice.... Time turned ... and passed ... and Luther baby girl Constance ... blessed with ... the Calling Up voice ... Ruth Bell ... baby girl ... Gayle Ann ... blessed ... with Emanuel... And time ... time pass ... es ... turns ... Emanuel .. will deliver us .. "

154

She fought to Tell it one last time. Her lips moved, but she was as voiceless as when she began. Finally her lips closed. There was only the oak-on-oak creak of the rocker against the floor.

Before fear registered, instinct made Gayle place her hand over Great's opened eyes.

Let Great stay in the chair, she instructed herself. Let the rocking stop on its own. Death wasn't so scary. Not the way old people die. Old people just pass into it. Like sunsets pass and seasons pass. Old folks know how to do it.

She couldn't leave the room. If she left she would have to reenter and find Miss Great in her rocker gone from this world. But if she stayed there with Great, talking the history, she would hear Miss Great's voice guiding hers through the Telling. If she walked in circles and chanted, Miss Great's body wouldn't be so still.

She didn't hear Miss Auntie and Uncle Luther coming up the stairs. She was chanting. She didn't hear them enter the room, though someone was calling her name. She couldn't hear them. She had to Tell, over and over, so she would have it in her.

Then she saw something. The black angel of death moved toward the rocker, picked up Miss Great's body, and laid her on the bed. Then a loud roar of pain broke Gayle from her dizzying chant. She saw her uncle crying at Miss Great's bedside. Miss Auntie rushed to the bed and threw herself around Uncle Luther. They cried on the bed like orphaned children while Gayle looked on.

Why didn't she feel their grief? She could see how it pulled their lips and cheeks into scary masks. She could hear it in their choking and sobbing. What she couldn't do was jump on the deathbed and join in crying, no matter how badly she wanted to.

Tell them, she thought. Tell them Miss Great up there in paradise, with her Lord and her Luther and her Sonny. Tell them.

Something stopped her. She felt another presence and turned to greet it. Before she could reach out to her cousin, Cookie fled without offering her sorrow.

❧ 22 ❧

THE NEXT MORNING Gayle lay on her bed with José teddy-beared within the curve of her body. Miss Auntie entered the room and sat at her side.

"Morning, Gayle."

Though awake, Gayle kept her eyes closed, hoping her aunt would go away.

"Don't you think it's time to stop hiding behind the baby?" her aunt asked. Gayle did not respond.

"Coroner came by, sweetie."

Finally she spoke. "Am I gon' to jail for that recipe?"

"No, sweetie," she said and pulled Gayle's thumb out of her mouth. "The coroner said the recipe let Great go peacefully."

Gayle wanted to believe her, but she couldn't tell if Miss Auntie was just being nice or being for real.

"You know she Told me."

"I know."

"Why'd she do that? She knew I'm no genius. Why she didn't Tell Uncle or you or Cookie? I know I got it in me somewhere, but I can't remember a word of it right now. I mean, that's our family history. 'Bout our freedom and all "

Her aunt's smile simply grew and grew. "If all you remember is how valuable our family history is, then you've got it all."

"But s'pose I lost it for good?"

"It'll come out when you're ready, sweetie. You'll do just fine."

"Miss Auntie, you always saying that."

"That's because I know you, Miss Gayle. You have good sense, like Great. It will all come together when you finish growing. Now, have some faith. Put some in God, some in yourself, and some in the people who love you. Give yourself a chance. You'll do just fine."

The joy of having the Telling along with all of Great's remembrances made Gayle suddenly talkative. She sat up.

"Miss Great told me lots of things."

"Like?"

"Her funeral. She wanted a big funeral like Old Luther and Sonny's with strong preaching and singers from Canaday."

"Canada."

Gayle shrugged. She could only repeat what she had heard. "Great said Canaday and lots of food. Lots of people in the house making it lively. And she don't want that high-neck dress in the gold bag. She wants a dress that reminds people she was young and happy."

"You helped get her ready?"

"She told me to."

"Gayle Ann, stop feeling so guilty. I'm asking you about covering the mirrors, facing Miss Abigail east."

"She told me to."

"That's old," Miss Auntie said. "Something folks don't do anymore." Her eyes watered. "We have lost a treasure in Miss Great, you know"

Gayle nodded.

"Bet you didn't know Miss Great helped me snag Luther."

"Oh, that love potion?" Gayle drawled. Then she listed the ingredients, the way Great had with rhymes and beats. Miss Auntie shook her head in disbelief, her face ready to break apart. Gayle wished she could take it back. She didn't mean to say the ingredients to the love potion. It just spilled right out.

Miss Auntie dried her eyes and stood up. "People will be by soon to pay their respects. Come on downstairs when you're ready."

Gayle put José into his wooden crib. She threw the quilt over him, realizing he wouldn't sleep much longer. He'd be hollering for his bath, his food, and for someone to play with. She looked down on him, wishing he could stay quiet and peaceful like that, wrapped under the quilt. He made such a picture. Him. The quilt. The squares in the corners. Two shells. The opened gate. The cotton that looked like clouds. The stump.

She let out a gasp. *As many times as José had wet that thing up! Didn't Cookie know that quilt belonged to the family? Wait till I tell her . . .*

Cookie wasn't interested in her discovery.

"Dog, Cookie. They didn't even put Great in the ground. You still broke up over Stacey. Don't you think you should be spilling some tears for Great?"

"Look who's talking. I don't see you crying."

"That's 'cause I know she really wanted to go to paradise. Besides, I got all this cooking and cleaning to do to help Miss Auntie with the wake. Things you should be doing."

"Great's gone. Nothing I can do to bring her back."

"But you can do something besides lying here mooning over Stacey."

"I'm doing something," Cookie said. "And I need your help."

"Now you talking."

"Tell them I'm sick and I want to go to bed early. Leave the back door unlatched and put my robe in the pantry so I can slip it on. If Daddy or Mommy come downstairs, I'll just say I wanted a snack."

"That's so stupid, Cookie. They'll hear your car coming and going unless Stacey's going to park way down from the house."

"He doesn't know I'm coming."

"Ain't you just too much. Hope you get your feelings hurt."

"I just need to talk to him," Cookie said.

Gayle rolled her eyes. "Save that lie for your mama. You all heated up and ready to go."

"So what if I am."

"Well scuse me, Cuz. I thought being saved was for real. I see the Holy Ghost fly out the window at the first crack."

Now Cookie rolled her eyes.

"Okay," Gayle said. "I'll unbolt the back door and put your robe in the pantry, if that's what you want."

"That's what I want."

"But you gotta do something I want. Go and say something nice to your daddy. Cookie, the way Uncle Luther cried at Miss Great's bed breaked my heart in two."

"Awright," Cookie said.

Unh-unh, Gayle noted. She couldn't trust Cookie to do the right thing. If Cookie was listening she would have said, "It's *broke* not *breaked*." Instead Cookie stared her down, full of her own will.

Uncle Luther went to the funeral parlor to make the arrangements while Miss Auntie called people on the

160

phone with news of Great. Gayle wondered if she'd be lying by smiling in Miss Auntie's face, knowing Cookie was up to no good. She decided it was better to stay out of Miss Auntie's way and keep her hands busy.

Folks from the South can show out, Gayle thought, taking stock of the tinfoiled casserole dishes and pans cradling pies, macaroni and cheese, cobblers, hams, and salads. Their donors had been blessed at one time or another by "Miss Abigail's" charity and patience. Each party came bearing a dish and their most amusing or strongest recollection of Abigail Coston Gates. Gayle was amazed by the outpour, but quickly fell into the spirit of the visitors, who were gracious, sorry, and cheerful all in one shot. Gayle never tired of repeating how Great went peacefully, looking toward paradise. It made everyone happy.

"Know what, Cook? You should put on some music. Some of that stuff you said your opera-loving grandma liked." Gayle would have said "our" but she had never seen the woman except in a picture frame. And in her mother's face.

"Papa don't like the stereo playing music. He uses it for his tapes."

"You still going, ain't you?"

"Soon's folks stop coming by."

"People come here asking for you. Turned your own mother into a liar talking about 'Cookie and Great was very close.'"

"We were."

Gayle put her hands on her hips. "You singing Great's burial?"

"I don't feel up to it."

"But you up to hopping into Stacey's bed."

161

"Leave me alone, Cousin."

"No problem, Cuz."

Cookie stomped into her room. Gayle went down the hall. It was the second time she had opened the door to Great's room only to be stopped by the empty bed. Instead of standing at the threshold, she entered this time, her arms wrapped tightly around her waist. Everything remained as it was. The mirrors were covered. The rocking chair faced east. The mason jar sat on the windowsill filling the room with its fragrance.

By late afternoon Miss Auntie became fed up with Cookie's rudeness and made her come downstairs and sit with the company. From what Gayle could see, Cookie still hadn't spoken to her daddy.

"Wish my daddy still living," Gayle told José as she fed him. "Cookie should be glad she got a daddy."

José agreed wholeheartedly. He grabbed the spoon from his mother and yelled, "Da-da-da-da-da-da."

By ten o'clock the house was quiet. Miss Auntie and Uncle Luther retired early. Miss Auntie said Uncle Luther didn't react well to death, though Gayle had already figured as much. Gayle could see Uncle Luther making that stone face as a boy driving his daddy's body home for burial. She could see him standing by as his daddy and granddaddy were lowered into the ground. Uncle Luther preached paradise, but his heart didn't leap toward it. Not like Great's heart before it finally gave out.

Gayle cleaned the coffee urns, put away the tins of food, and wiped down the kitchen. She was mopping when she heard footsteps behind her.

It was Cookie, face swollen with stubbornness. So swollen her mouth wouldn't open to speak as she tramped across the damp tile.

162

"Wait," Gayle said as Cookie went out the back door.

"Go back, Cousin," Cookie said, heading straight for her car.

Gayle followed. "Thought you was saved, Cookie."

"Leave me alone, Cousin."

"And what if I don't?" Gayle asked.

"I'll make you," Cookie told her.

Gayle ran ahead and planted herself against the car door. Cookie was coming at her.

"Go through me, you so bad," Gayle dared.

Cookie said plainly, "I don't want to hurt you," and kept coming, keys jingling in her hand.

"You the one gon' get hurt," Gayle bluffed, holding her ground. Hadn't she tussled with Mama? She could handle Cookie.

All Gayle knew was a second ago she was on her feet. That second was all Cookie needed to jam the key into the door. Gayle picked herself up and latched onto Cookie before she could get the door open. With one foot dug in the dirt and the other against the car door, Gayle grunted and pulled against Cookie's weight. Cookie was immovable and determined to get inside her car. She didn't have time for fooling around and ended it altogether, sending Gayle back down in the dirt, this time flat out on her back. Gayle reached out for the tire to steady herself, but instead felt something round. It was the mason jar she had emptied earlier.

Gayle heard the accelerator being pumped and smelled the fumes that sputtered from the exhaust. Curious peachy mixture. She sprang up out of the dirt and ran to the driver's window, beating her fist against the glass.

"You s'posed to be saved, Cookie! I know you hear me."

The engine *ssssshhhh*red.

Cookie shook her head to drown out her cousin. She

shook the steering wheel and pumped the accelerator relentlessly. The engine shrieked before it gave out completely.

"I know you hear me, Cuz. Let me save you. Just let me save you." Gayle's mouth opened. She tried to say it again—"Let me save you"—but could only mouth it. Something choked her, deep in her throat. It choked and choked and choked, then broke through. Tears. Down her eyes, her nose, her mouth. A mess. Just a mess. She couldn't stop crying.

The car door opened and she fell in alongside Cookie. They sat and cried and cried hot tears long before either could speak.

"Let me save you, Cuz," Gayle said. "Just let me save you."

"Who," Cookie sniffled, "gonna save you, Cuz?"

"Yawl," Gayle sobbed. "All yawl."

From their lighted window neither Miss Auntie nor Uncle Luther could make out who was leading whom back to the house. But something about the smell of fermented peaches in the air told them that both girls were finally home

Homegirl,

What up? Don't think I havn't forgot the
letter you never sen me. So much hapen since
my last letter.
Great had her a big blow-out funral lik she always
wanted. Mama came and Mama and Cookie
sang Great into the ground somthing nice. I
never cryd so much. It was butiful. Mama and
Junie staying. Uncle Luther grumbel but Miss
Auntie got her way. Cookie and Stacie holdng
hands at the funral. Girl, he stick on her like
glue. Disgusting. The baby try to walk and
talk. He gots a mouth full of teef.

Mama say shell watch the baby if I go to
school. Miss Auntie say I can stay home and
work in the house if I want to. Miss Auntie aint
slick and I aint stupid. I'm gon to school. Beats
being a house slave.

Yawl shud come on down. Its so nice.

Peace,

Gayle

Rita Williams-Garcia grew up in Seaside, California, and Jamaica, New York. She is also the author of the novels *Blue Tights* (Puffin) and *Fast Talk on a Slow Track*, an ALA Best Book for Young Adults and recipient of a Special Citation from the PEN/Norma Klein Committee.

Rita Williams-Garcia lives in Jamaica, New York. She has two daughters.